SARCOMA:
The Demon Inside

By:
Samantha R. Bond

The name's Bond. Samantha Bond. I inherited it by marrying my sweet, handsome, and talented husband, Bobby Carl Bond Jr. Over the years, we've both been teased about the name. But the purpose of this book is not about that—it's to tell our story, to share our journey and the experiences we've had in life and marriage.

At first, I planned to write this book on my own. When I first told my husband about it, he said, "No," and I was crushed. Writing and becoming a published author has always been a dream of mine, inspired by so many authors who have come before me. I have so much to share.

After a week of reflection, the desire to write didn't fade. It's something I've always wanted. As a teenager and into my early twenties, I turned to poetry to express my emotions. Writing was therapeutic; it allowed me to release feelings that I couldn't voice out loud when I felt no one else would listen.

But I respected my husband's feelings, so I asked him again. This time, I sent him a heartfelt plea via text, saying, "I'm just going to say this once. It has always been my dream to be a published author. I believe this book could be a remarkable success and help so many people in countless ways. Yes, it's personal, but so many successful authors share the 'nitty-gritty' details of their lives."

While sitting in the driveway, waiting for him to pull up, he called me. I explained the text briefly over the phone, asking him to just hear me out. I told him how much it would mean to me to write our story— not just to fulfill my dream but to help others and glorify God in the process. After listening, he agreed. And so, here I am, writing.

This book will tell the true story of the past three years and all we've experienced. It's meant to help anyone facing similar struggles and raise awareness about mental health, God's protection, and even demonic oppression. I use the word "oppression" because, unlike possession, it refers to being influenced, attacked, or weighed down by dark spiritual forces without them fully taking control. This can manifest in emotional, mental, or even physical challenges, making life feel overwhelming at times. Above all, this book aims to glorify God. And, of course, there are some surprises along the way!

CONTENTS

ACKNOWLEDGEMENTS 1

THE BEGINNING 2

JUMPING TO JUNE OF 2020 4

END OF JUNE 2020 7

SUMMER 2020 8

AUGUST 2020 9

SAD MOMENTS 10

THE WEIGHT ON MY SHOULDERS ON THE WAY BACK
TO SUFFOLK 12

BOBBY'S REHABILITATION AND ARRIVAL HOME 13

TRAUMA 14

BEGINNING PARTS OF 2021 17

SPILLING MORE INTO 2021, IT WAS A BIG BLUR, FORGIVE
ME 19

DUKE VISITS 21

NEAR THE END OF 2021 22

JANUARY 2022 25

SPIRITUAL GIFT'S 26

EASTER 2022 My anointing 28

DEMONS IN THE BIBLE 30

MANIC 2022 32

HOSPITALIZATION DIARIES 34

    8/15/2022 34

    8/17/2022 34

    8/18/2022 36

    Thursday Afternoon 36

    Friday 8/19/2022 37

Friday Continued…. 39

Saturday 8-20-2022 40

Saturday Evening Continued…… 41

Sunday 8/21/2022 43

MY SECRET ANCESTRY 45

BACK TO HOSPITALIZATION DIARIES 47

Sunday Afternoon, 8/21/2022 47

Sunday evening 8/21/22 48

Monday 8/22/22 49

Tuesday 8/23/2022 50

THINGS WE TAKE FOR GRANTED 52

Tuesday continued.. 52

8/24/2022 Wednesday 53

Wednesday Afternoon 54

Thursday 55

Friday 8/26/2022 56

8/27/2022 Saturday 57

Sunday 8/28/2022 58

Sunday continued 58

Monday 8/29/2022 59

Tuesday 8/30/2022 60

Wednesday, 8/31/2022 61

Thursday 9/1/22022 61

Friday 9/2/2022 – Lucas's birthday 62

Saturday 9/3/2022 63

Sunday 9/4/2022 63

9/5/2022 64

Tuesday 9/6/2022 64

Wednesday 9/7/2022 64

Thursday 9/8/2022..65

Friday 9/9/2022...65

Saturday 9/10/2022...65

9/11/2022..66

9/12/2022..66

9/13/2022..66

Wednesday, 9/14/2022..66

Thursday, 9/15/2022...66

Friday, 9/16/2022..67

Saturday, 9/17/2022..67

Sunday, 9/18/2022...67

RETURNING HOME FROM THE MENTAL HEALTH
INSTITUTE..69

2023 - Attempting To Get Back To Normalcy 69

June...72

Self-Care 101 72

Art Therapy..73

August/September 2023 74

Christmas 2023 74

2024 - RECOVERY AND REDEMPTION YEAR 75

Protecting my peace...77

3/3/2024 Lucas's Baptism...79

Timo, Timo, Timo! 81

Encouraging the community on group..83

Proud of Bobby 83

Therapy Today 3/2024...84

It's Called Spiritual Growth, Baby Girl!...85

TGIF 85

My Favorite Poem..86

St. Patty's Day Eviction.. 86

Cards In The Mail 87

Being A Good Samaratin 87

Bobby's Body Now... 88

3/21 88

Middle Of The Night Entry 89

Saturday March 23... 90

Hope on Palm Sunday 91

Monday 92

Poem For Bobby, Honoring Christina Perry's 1000 Years & Also Our Wedding Song 94

Easter Sunday 2024.. 95

April Fool's Day 95

Friday April 5th 95

Sunday, April 21 99

Satan loves to attack our minds. 102

Just another manic Monday.. 102

MY 3 P's.. 104

Prayer 104

Positivity 104

Perseverance... 104

Tuesday 5/14 105

5/19/2024 105

Bobby's Surgery 5/20 106

Torture Tuesday 106

The Middle Of The Week... 107

Sunday 5/26 108

Wednesday 5/29.. 108

Saturday, June 1st 108

Tyranny Tuesday 109

A couple of days later 110

Tough Cookie 111

7 June, My birthday 111

6/9/2024 112

Monday 113

Wednesday 6/12/24 113

Father's Day weekend 114

JESUS IS OUR LIGHTHOUSE 116

ABOUT THE AUTHOR 118

ACKNOWLEDGEMENTS

Firstly, I would like to thank our Heavenly Father for giving me life and all my gifts and for giving His only begotten son, Jesus Christ, who died on the cross to save me from my sins.

Thank you to my husband, Bobby Carl Bond Jr., for sticking it out through thick and thin, for better or worse, in sickness and in health, for richer or poorer, as long as we both shall live!

Thank you to my parents, Sharon and Bobby Winslow, for supporting us financially through the past few years. I know it has not been easy for any of us, but God's love shines brightly through both of you as you have watched over us and guided us through this challenging time in our lives.

Thank you to my best friend, Brooke Scott, for being legendary, for being a true friend, for loving me through the darkness, and for believing in me even when I couldn't believe in myself.

Thank you to my two brothers in Christ from Africa, Vahe Christopher Hubert and Timo Fakoson, for loving me from afar and supporting me through prayer and encouragement.

Thank you to my favorite authors, J.K. Rowling, Nicholas Sparks, and Stephenie Meyer, for being an inspiration in my life. Thank you also to Trent Shelton for having such a big impact on my daily walk and being an inspiration.

Finally, thank you to the rest of my family, friends, acquaintances, and fellow church members for supporting us through prayer, finances, encouragement, and love over the past few years.

THE BEGINNING

It was the year 2020, and many of us had high hopes that it would be a wonderful year. Unfortunately, we were wrong. Little did we know, our worst nightmare was just around the corner. In March, we made the decision to move back in with my parents. We had to break our lease at the apartment complex we were living in, citing a medical emergency. That was partly true because Bobby, my husband, had been suffering from severe pain in his lower back. But honestly, we just couldn't afford the rent anymore, along with the payments for Lucas, our son's preschool. We were way over our heads despite both of us working hard.

Lucas was attending preschool at a local Christian academy, but the cost was becoming unmanageable. At one point, we considered moving in with Bobby's grandmother. But when I mentioned it to my mom, she immediately said, "No, just move back in with us." She was thinking of her grandson's wellbeing, and in hindsight, it wouldn't have been the best choice to move in with his grandmother anyway. Her house was in poor shape, with cigarette smoke stains covering the walls from years of heavy smoking. You could literally wipe your finger on the wall and see the residue. The walls had a dingy, brownish-yellow tint to them, and it was honestly filthy. Even though she'd been on oxygen for a while, she continued to smoke, which worried us. We wanted Lucas to see her more, but we couldn't bring ourselves to have him around all that smoke. We knew how harmful secondhand smoke could be.

Then, almost as soon as we moved in with my mom and stepdad, Covid happened! I had only been working as a supervisor at a local grocery chain for about six months when the virus hit, and no one knew what to make of it. This new virus, which primarily attacked the respiratory system and caused flu-like symptoms, began spreading rapidly across the country and the world. It was a scary time, and nobody knew what to expect. Soon, government officials and the CDC were urging everyone to wear masks, and everything at work changed overnight.

It was a terrifying period for everyone—doctors, nurses, teachers, business owners—no one was spared from the anxiety and uncertainty. We did our best to follow the guidelines as a family, though we didn't go to extreme measures as some did. Not that being extra cautious was wrong, but we didn't isolate ourselves in separate rooms or wear masks at home. However, if a business required masks, we complied. Bobby and I both hated wearing them, as did many people, but what really got to me was seeing Lucas having to wear a mask at school. It felt so unnatural, especially knowing that masks restrict your breathing and you're inhaling your own carbon dioxide along with bacteria.

"Be alert and of sober mind. Your enemy, the devil, prowls around like a roaring lion looking for someone to devour." **1 Peter 5:8**

Looking back, Covid sent the entire world into a state of shock, fear, and isolation. From a Christian perspective, it felt like the perfect tool for the enemy to use—isolating families, spreading despair, making people sick, causing them to lose faith in God, and even leading some to suicide or forced compliance. The whole experience was overwhelming for everyone.

At the time, Bobby was working five days a week at his construction job, along with a part-time job that I had helped him land. He really enjoyed that job and was doing so well that they were even considering promoting him to an area manager. His role involved taking photographs on construction sites for safety documentation. Bobby had been losing some weight from all his hard work, but none of us thought much of it.

We had also noticed a small lump on his inner right thigh, but we assumed it was just some sort of swelling. At night, he struggled to sleep, constantly tossing and turning because he couldn't get comfortable. He often complained about his lower back and hip pain, but I didn't realize just how much pain he was really in. Eventually, he made an appointment to see a spine specialist. They did a scan and saw that something was off, but they couldn't pinpoint exactly what it was. I remember even a physician's assistant looked at the lump on his thigh and didn't seem concerned at the time. Reflecting on it now, I can't help but feel like a PA or doctor should have recognized that something wasn't right.

JUMPING TO JUNE OF 2020

Though I can't recall the exact day, I remember it vividly. I had woken up early that morning to get ready for work. Bobby had been working at his construction job, and it was taking a toll on his body. He had been in pain for quite some time, especially in his lower back and hip, which made sleeping nearly impossible. He would toss and turn all night, and it kept me awake, too. Despite being tough, the pain was relentless—he would come home complaining almost every day.

That particular morning, I remember waking him up so he wouldn't be late for work. He needed to go to the bathroom, but as he stood up, he nearly collapsed in pain. He sat down on the toilet, clutching his lower abdomen in agony. He tried to urinate but couldn't. I rushed into the bathroom, alarmed, and asked him what was wrong. He told me he was in excruciating pain and unable to urinate. At that moment, I knew something was seriously wrong.

I immediately called my manager to say I wouldn't be coming in and told them I had to take Bobby to the emergency room. I remember talking to my Aunt Arden before we left, and she suggested we go to urgent care to save money. But I ignored her advice and trusted my instincts—I took him straight to the hospital.

When we arrived, the nurses initially thought Bobby had kidney stones, suspecting that his pain was coming from that. Thankfully, they decided to run some scans. They let Bobby lie down in a bed and gave him pain medication while we waited for the results. I was told I could grab something to eat while we waited, so I headed down to the cafeteria. As I sat there, I heard God speak clearly to me—one word: "Cancer." My heart sank. Deep down, I knew we were facing something severe.

I returned to the room and updated everyone with a photo of Bobby in the E.R. Just then, the physician's assistant came rushing in, looking deeply concerned. He said, "You've got a sarcoma in your pelvis, a massive one!" I was confused and thought to myself, *What is a sarcoma?* He explained that it was a cancerous tumor and that it was pressing on Bobby's organs, causing issues with his bladder and other complications.

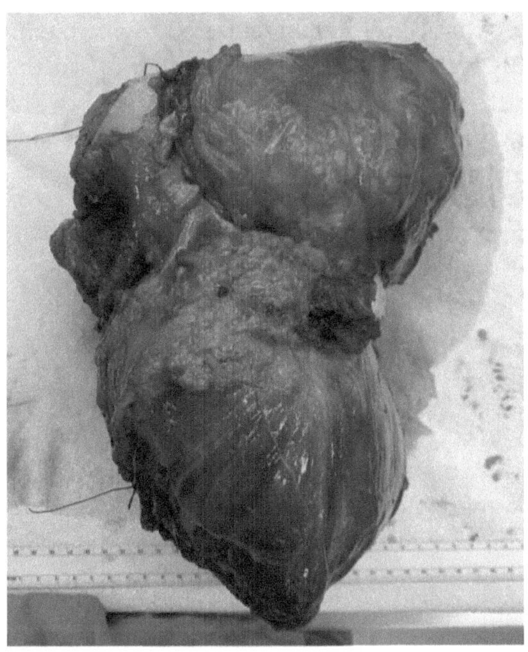

They kept Bobby overnight for observation, and I went home to get some rest. My parents were anxious to know what was happening. As I hugged them, I said, "Either Bobby will live, or he'll be in heaven with Jesus." I didn't know what else to say. The hospital had contacted a specialist in Virginia Beach who dealt with cases like Bobby's, and within a week, we went to that appointment.

At first, I was optimistic about meeting the specialist, hoping they had a plan for him. They had even reached out to Johns Hopkins. But when the doctor explained the situation, it became clear there weren't many options. The tumor was enormous, inside his pelvis, and attached to his pelvic bone and right hip joint. It extended through his pelvis and was even attached along his inner thigh muscle. Johns Hopkins had reviewed the case and couldn't see any other way to remove it except by amputating Bobby's leg.

Bobby and I sat in that office, holding each other's hands, trying to process everything the doctor was telling us. We left the appointment heartbroken. We walked to the car and just sat there, sobbing in each other's arms. We were devastated.

Of all people, my husband was the one with this rare form of cancer.

We truly believe that he was being targeted by the enemy. This wasn't from God. This was a disease—a demonic entity in the valley of the shadow of death—that had been attacking his body, creeping up on him slowly and undetected. It was like a wolf in sheep's clothing, sneaky and deceptive.

"For we are not fighting against flesh- and blood- enemies. Finally, be strong in the Lord and his mighty power. Put on the full armor of God so that you stand against the devil's schemes. For our struggle is not against flesh and blood, but against the rulers, against the authorities, against the power of this dark world, and against the spiritual forces of evil in the heavenly realms." Ephesians 6: 10-12

We were convinced that the devil had planted one of his schemes in our lives—to destroy Bobby's body, to sever our connection with the Lord, to break apart our marriage, and to tear down our family. And this was only the beginning of the horror that awaited us.

That afternoon, I called Arden in tears and told her everything. She immediately apologized for suggesting we go to urgent care instead of the hospital—she had only been trying to save us money. She rallied up prayer groups and was just as devastated as we were by the news. In her usual dramatic fashion, she threw herself into helping, and I loved her for that. Her caring and compassionate nature always shined through, and I've always taken after her in the drama department!

My mom and stepfather heard from a family member that we should get a second opinion before moving forward with Johns Hopkins' recommendation. Thank God for second opinions! We discovered that Duke University Hospital, a teaching hospital, had a dedicated Sarcoma team. They may be called the Duke Blue Devils, but they should really be called the Duke Angels. Their angelic spirit and what the whole university stands for truly amazed us.

The entire team at Duke was so kind, compassionate, and incredibly helpful. I have nothing but the highest praise for Duke University Hospital and its Sarcoma team.

END OF JUNE 2020

Bobby and I made the three-hour drive from Suffolk down to Durham, NC. It was a straight shot, but it felt like such a long drive, especially given the weight of what we were facing. It was late June. When we arrived at Duke University Hospital, we opted for valet parking, and I'm so glad we did. Duke is huge, and there was a lot of walking involved, which Bobby was already struggling with because of all the pain he was in.

There were people everywhere, walking to their destinations—going to classes, various buildings, work, or offices. We had to make our way down to level one. As we walked through the hospital, I noticed a pianist playing softly, filling the space with beautiful music. It was such a pleasant sound. The walls were adorned with various paintings—scenes of nature and people by rivers, all of which I loved because I'm a fan of art. It felt peaceful, even for a cancer center.

Bobby's nurse practitioner and surgeon were absolutely amazing! His surgeon was incredibly humble, giving credit to her entire team rather than taking it for herself. Thankfully, they had a plan, and they were ready to act fast. They wanted to get that sarcoma—what we referred to as a "demon"—out of him as soon as possible so it wouldn't have more time to grow or damage his organs.

The best news came when the surgeon expressed confidence in saving Bobby's leg, which was music to his ears. I remember him, in a moment of anger, saying, "I'm keeping my leg, dammit!" Even though I'm not fond of cursing, I let him express his emotions—I knew how much this meant to him.

The surgeon explained that they would need to perform a hemi-pelvectomy, which meant they would have to remove the sarcoma along with half of his right pelvic bone and his right hip joint. We asked if there was any option for a metal replacement to repair the loss, but his surgeon recommended against it. She explained that keeping a flailed pelvis was the best choice, as reopening him and placing something foreign in his body would pose a high risk of infection. The last thing we wanted was to risk that.

SUMMER 2020

Prior to Bobby's surgery, my grandfather had a holistic approach, almost like a cancer regimen, for Bobby to follow before treatment, so we did what he suggested. It was a mixture of all sorts of good things for the body. Bobby was also trying to eat healthily and was juicing every day. Since Bobby was out of work, he needed something to occupy his time, so he found solace in gardening. He got good exercise out in the garden and a real bronze tan—he looked very handsome! To me, Bobby looked like a Roman or Greek soldier, just without all the armor, lol! Looking at him, you wouldn't think he had cancer at all. Bobby just focused on his gardening until it was time for his surgery. For him, getting out in the sunshine and working in the dirt was the best medicine.

AUGUST 2020

It was time for the surgery. Thankfully, I had raised enough charity money through Facebook to stay home with Bobby for seven weeks. Without that money, I wouldn't have been able to. I was very grateful for every one of our family and friends who donated during our time of need. One kind family member even helped pay for my hotel room while Bobby was in the hospital, so I had a place to stay while I waited. Since it was the middle of COVID, I couldn't wait in the hospital for Bobby to get out of surgery, so I waited in my room, patiently waiting to hear from his surgeon. It was kind of miserable. While waiting in my hotel room, I received text messages every hour saying "surgery continues" over and over, and then I finally got one that said "surgery complete." It felt very impersonal and unnerving.

Finally, around 10 p.m., I got a call from his surgeon, who told me Bobby was awake and doing very well. He said Bobby's surgery was a success and had the best possible outcome. The tumor hadn't attached itself to his organs, so they were able to save all of them, meaning he didn't need a colostomy bag or tubes or anything like that.

SAD MOMENTS

The saddest part of this journey was the night before Bobby's surgery when we made love for what turned out to be the last time. As a married couple, we had no idea it would be our final moment of intimacy. When I say the Devil knocked Bobby's dick in the dirt, he really did! The heartbreaking thing was that sexual intimacy was Bobby and I's love language. We truly enjoyed physical touch and connection, and it was stolen from us, like taking candy from a child or a pacifier from a baby. It was gone—completely disconnected. The tumor had attached itself to Bobby's genitals from the inside, and they had to remove that part, causing significant nerve damage. The devil had his schemes, planning to ruin our marriage because he knew our connection, our love for each other, was powerful. The devil comes to steal, kill, and destroy, and his schemes have killed Bobby's self-esteem and self-confidence, making him feel like less of a man.

We all know that part of a man's confidence comes from being able to perform in the bedroom and make his partner happy. But the damage went beyond that—it also tore down his self-confidence as a provider. The sarcoma had suddenly made him disabled for the rest of his life. They had to remove half of his pelvic bone and his right hip joint. Bobby became very sad and bitter inside because he didn't feel adequate to be the provider he wanted to be.

The next morning, I finally got to see Bobby after surgery. It was a heartbreaking moment, seeing my husband helpless in bed, drugged up and with a bedpan. He was hooked up to IVs and had a spinal IV for pain management. The nurses did a great job taking care of him, giving him everything he needed, but he just lay there watching *Alien* with Sigourney Weaver. I sat in the corner, keeping him company, reading a book, and staying close in case he needed anything or wanted me to call a nurse. His mom had come to be with me during the surgery, but since it was the middle of COVID, only one family member was allowed to visit him in the hospital. Unfortunately, she had to leave early because I, as his wife, was his next of kin. It made me sad that she didn't get to see her firstborn son after such a traumatic event, but I did my best to keep my composure. What else could I do?

I know many people went through similar experiences, unable to visit loved ones in hospitals or nursing homes because of COVID and all the restrictions. It was disheartening, and it simply wasn't fair.

THE WEIGHT ON MY SHOULDERS ON THE WAY BACK TO SUFFOLK

Suddenly, I found myself in a position where I felt I needed to be the sole provider for our family. Here I was, a woman with a disabled husband and a 4-year-old son to take care of, all by myself. I was frightened. I didn't know what to do. On the drive home from the hospital, I did my best to focus on the road, and then I clearly heard God in my mind say, "Be still and know that I am God." I tried my best to hold onto that voice, but it faded away quickly. All I could think about was getting home to see Lucas. He needed me. He hadn't seen his momma in a week, and he hadn't seen his daddy either.

BOBBY'S REHABILITATION AND ARRIVAL HOME

Bobby was transported from Duke University Hospital to a rehabilitation center in Newport News, about a 40-minute drive from Suffolk. It wasn't too far, but still a bit of a drive. He stayed there for two whole weeks and received excellent care. Since he was closer, I was able to visit him more often. He even said the food was much tastier than what he had at the hospital. They put him through several physical therapy activities, mostly focusing on strengthening his upper body, which he was going to need. They helped rehabilitate him as best as they could.

After being discharged, Bobby needed a wheelchair. The staff showed me how to operate it and how to help him in and out of it. He also had a wound vac, and they gave me detailed instructions on how to manage it, which was quite confusing, but I did my best to pay attention. Thankfully, my stepfather's side of the family pitched in and built a wooden wheelchair ramp attached to the back porch of our house. That was a huge help, and I was truly grateful for their kindness.

When Bobby arrived home, getting him out of the car was a real challenge. It was hard to transfer him from the backseat to the wheelchair, but I managed. I wheeled him up the wooden ramp, and Lucas was excited to see his dad. However, he didn't understand what was going on or why his daddy was in a wheelchair and couldn't walk. We had explained to him that Daddy had a very large boo-boo that the doctors had to remove and that it would stop him from walking for a while. But his innocent mind couldn't quite grasp the bigger picture.

The wheelchair caused a lot of scuffing on the walls and doorways—it was wide, and the doorways were narrow, so squeezing through was tricky. Bobby would be in a wheelchair for six months and would have to learn how to walk all over again. The weight of it all was on my shoulders. I had vowed to stay by my husband's side in sickness and in health, and now it was up to me to take care of him.

TRAUMA

Bobby came home with 200 staples in him. His wound was significant. It wrapped around his waist and extended into his groin, and there was even an incision on his inner thigh. When I say it looked like a great white shark had attacked him and bitten him in half, it really did. The surgeons had to literally filet Bobby from the waist down to remove that 10-pound demon. When I talk about trauma, I truly experienced it. If you're not used to seeing graphic things happen to someone you love, it weighs heavily on your mind. His wounds weren't healed; they were still open, and there was a big hole in the crease of his groin that I had to pack with silver ribbon for months. I even prayed that it would close as a Christmas gift, but it didn't. The hole was deep.

Since Bobby couldn't get his wounds wet, I had to give him sponge baths periodically. I'll admit, I didn't bathe him as much as I should have. I was busy working and taking care of Lucas, too. Looking back, I should have asked for more help. I should have prayed more. I should have used more resources for guidance, but I didn't. I felt completely alone.

We were grateful for the charity we received because it allowed me to stay home and ensure Bobby was getting plenty of protein. But he wasn't getting enough fiber, which led to complications with going to the bathroom. The medications he was on blocked his bowels, so we used prunes and prune juice to help. We had applied for financial aid through Duke because there was no way we could afford his surgery— it was a quarter-of-a-million-dollar operation. Thankfully, we were approved. Thank the Lord that Arden had told me about that!

The medical insurance from the grocery chain I worked for also helped cover most of the costs. Our healthcare system really needs improvement, especially for people in difficult situations or those living in poverty. Cancer is devastating, and it cripples everyone involved. Those who go through cancer treatment suffer from so many symptoms—brain fog, fatigue, weakness, and more. Everyone should have access to care without the burden of worrying about medical bills in situations like ours.

Bobby's cancer affected me deeply. I suffered from PTSD because of it. Insomnia set in, and I would wake up in the middle of the night, unable to go back to sleep, filled with fear and anxiety. I tried going downstairs, where my mom sat, and we'd watch Harry Potter together. Those marathons always brought me comfort. I should have been in constant prayer, but I wasn't. The spirit was willing, but the flesh was weak. It felt like the devil himself had come into the night, like a thief, and taken over my mind. I began to have suicidal thoughts, and as much as it pains me to admit, even dark, homicidal thoughts about my family.

I had become opressed by a demonic force. I started planning my suicide. I took my gun out of the closet and held it to my temple, imagining driving to my childhood home and ending my life in front of it, leaving others to find me in my car, dead. I heard voices in my head telling me that I was suffering out of love and asking why I should let those around me suffer, too. They used the word "love." I battled within myself—how could that be love? It wasn't. I was being tricked by demons.

Demons prey on the weak-minded and brokenhearted. They feed on our souls, draining every bit of joy, happiness, and laughter. They serve Satan, and they never sleep. They are always prowling, looking to devour anyone they can. I had become, in a sense, a zombie. The devil had convinced me that I would be destitute and starve to death. I began hoarding food, buying extra groceries, and stocking up on beans and canned goods as if the world were coming to an end. My mother assured me we weren't going to starve. How could we? The freezer was full. The cabinets were stocked. We had plenty, even enough to share with others. But I didn't believe her. I had gained 30 pounds, hoarding food like a squirrel preparing for winter. In my mind, the world was ending, and I was preparing for it.

I was so consumed by fear that I began chanting, "There's nothing I can do, there's nothing I can do, there's nothing I can do." I was definitely oppressed by a demonic force. My thoughts were not my own. It felt like Samantha had completely vanished.

I confessed my dark thoughts to Bobby, and he listened. I have no idea what he was thinking at the time, but I'm sure he was extremely worried, especially for the safety of our son. He told my mom about me having the gun and how I wasn't in a good state of mind. So my mom came upstairs, asked where my gun was, and locked it up in the safe.

BEGINNING PARTS OF 2021

My aunt Arden became very ill sometime between January and February with pneumonia, so she went to the doctor, and they gave her antibiotics to help clear it up. It was standard treatment for pneumonia, but she wasn't healing, so they wanted to do more tests. That's when Arden found out she had stage 4 lung cancer. Initially, they told her that with treatment, she had nine months to live. Unfortunately, in her case, that wasn't so.

I remember scaring my aunt by sharing my dark thoughts and voicing my fears about the end of time. She didn't know what to think, but she was still trying to be the loving aunt she always was, encouraging me to pray and read my Bible. But I wasn't listening to her. Satan is the father of all lies, and I believed everything he was feeding me. I wasn't listening to my aunt, and I wasn't relying on the Lord. I wasn't present—I was under oppression.

Some people may not believe in spiritual oppression, but I'm here to tell you that it's real. The Bible says so. Jesus healed many people who were oppressed by dark spiritual forces.

I'm so grateful for my good friend of 20 years, John. He saved me when I was in that dark place. Even though my thoughts were frightening, he remained faithful and listened intently as a true friend. I can't express how thankful I am for his friendship.

During my insomnia, I developed the habit of co-sleeping with Lucas. It was comforting for both of us, so I did it. Holding my child through the night gave me comfort—I needed him more than he needed me. As parents, we often forget to mention how much we need our children. After all, they are gifts from the Lord. Special gifts are given to us to teach us new things and to love. I needed my son's energy and love to keep me alive. I was so scared of losing him that I held him tightly.

I've constantly battled the idea of handing him over to my mom or my brother and his wife. Deep down, I knew I wasn't being the mother he needed me to be—I was sick. I was under oppression from a dark spiritual force, and while doctors might label it as a mental illness, I believe the two are closely linked.

Mental health issues run strongly in my family, particularly on my father's side. My grandfather, James Reed, was a believer in Jesus, but he struggled with his own sickness. He was a pharmaceutical salesman, and he began mixing medications with alcohol. When my dad was just 12 years old, my grandfather committed suicide, leaving my grandmother with four children to raise on her own.

My grandma did the best she could, given the circumstances. She was a registered nurse and worked night shifts, often relying on neighbors to check in on my uncle, my dad, and my aunts while she was at work. Pansy "Pat" Reed was tough; she had to be. She didn't have another choice. But my grandfather's suicide left our family in turmoil. It placed a generational curse on us.

Every member of our family was affected; it trickled down the line like a domino effect. My father suffered from mental health issues and self-medicated with alcohol for years, which led to my parents' divorce. Their separation impacted me deeply. Without a suitable father figure, my mom had to take on the role of both mother and father. She did her best, but it was hard, especially since she worked full-time.

SPILLING MORE INTO 2021, IT WAS A BIG BLUR, FORGIVE ME

While Bobby was at home recovering from his surgery, I fixed his meals for him, bathed him, and helped him put on his clothes. I dressed his wound every day, and we had nurses coming in to check on him, making sure his wound was healing properly. They did their best to help with his wound vac, but honestly, Bobby needed more care than what he received. We should have had a nurse come daily instead of once a week or every other week, but my insurance didn't cover home health care. I did everything I could, but it wasn't enough.

A man came to ask Bobby questions about his physical condition and when his therapy would begin. He was kind but not very helpful. Bobby started therapy at Sentara's therapy center by the YMCA, and I took him once a week. He was supposed to go twice a week, but I couldn't manage to take him both times. We should have asked someone for help with that, too.

Bobby's team at Duke was very concerned about my well-being and mental health. I was showing signs of poor behavior and mood. I had become extremely disconnected, depressed, and bitter inside. I was angry. I was bitter that I now had a disabled husband. I was angry that I had to take care of him. I was bitter that he couldn't walk. For better or for worse, in sickness and in health—this was our reality. I didn't like it one bit. In a way, I had become very selfish, only thinking of myself and the things that I felt had been stolen from me. The life I had pictured for us had diminished. Our dreams were crushed.

Even though I stayed by my husband's side, I wasn't truly honoring him. I wasn't there to encourage him or cheer him on, or even uplift him. I was so consumed by my own depression that I emotionally abandoned him. We were one, but I wasn't really there. I had left him alone in his healing process. When I took him to physical therapy, I would sulk like a child, crouching down and waiting impatiently. I wasn't the wife he needed me to be. He learned how to walk again all on his own. The Lord helped him regain his strength and gave him the courage to do the impossible. By wintertime, I had become cold and frigid.

Reflecting on this now, I feel guilty about my past actions. I can only ask for forgiveness for what I did or didn't do during that time. It is hard to forgive ourselves. That is probably the hardest thing—to forgive yourself when you find yourself in certain situations. I pray that God forgives me for not honoring Him because part of honoring the Lord is honoring your spouse. I pray for forgiveness of my sins.

DUKE VISITS

We would go every three months, making the three-hour drive from Suffolk to Durham, NC, to visit his team for scans and to make sure they were clean. The first few times were extremely difficult for me because Bobby couldn't walk, so he had to lie in the back seat, which was very uncomfortable for him. Then, upon arrival, I'd have to get the wheelchair out for him, but valet parking made things a bit easier.

NEAR THE END OF 2021

Bobby and my mom suggested that I look for another job because I was miserable at the grocery store. So, of course, I plugged away on Indeed, searching for something different. Eventually, I found a new opportunity and landed a job at a local mattress retailer. I thought, "I can sell mattresses; how hard could it be?" I remember sitting in the computer room with my mom and Bobby, and they noticed I wasn't speaking. When I go quiet, that's how you know something is very wrong with me—otherwise, I'm a sociable, chatty Kathy.

They said, "You've let the devil in this house!" It was a scary thought, but in a way, I had. Not intentionally, of course, but his presence and his influence seemed to linger around. Bobby was able to walk by then, and I could start to worry about him going up and down the staircase. Thankfully, he hadn't fallen because a fall would be detrimental. Even today, it would be disastrous if he were to fall. His upper body supports his lower body, and he walks with a cane. He can't walk long distances or run, and he gets exhausted easily since it takes so much energy to use his leg. His femur has found a spot in his scar tissue, but it rubs together, and eventually, it may give out.

Switching jobs did help me show some improvement. I left the toxic environment behind and moved to a quieter place with fewer people. People don't buy mattresses as often as they buy groceries. Still, I was deeply depressed. I wasn't getting the help I needed, and I wasn't listening to my family.

Anyways, I felt like I heard the voice of God in my head telling me, "Get to work, Samantha!" So, even though I was still getting over being sick and working at the mattress store, I had been looking for another source of income. I went on Zip Recruiter and that's where I found this company, kind of like GoodRx but slightly different. I got hired right away, and they assigned me a territory. I got to set my own hours, and I visited surrounding pharmacies.

Looking back now, Bobby probably should have put me in a mental health hospital that year because I was going through a very low mania, which is severe clinical depression. I wasn't sleeping well, I wasn't taking care of myself, and I had gained weight. I wasn't showering, and it's really depressing when your own family tells you that you stink and need to take a shower. But I refused. I didn't care. I wasn't wearing makeup or cute clothes that used to make me feel better. All the normal self-care things that people do, I was neglecting. My self-confidence and self-esteem had plummeted. Dark thoughts were consuming my mind.

I started believing we were going to be homeless because we were poor. Here I was, 37 years old, earning minimum wage with a disabled husband, living with my parents. It was easy for the devil's schemes to make me believe that this was our fate. I was even reading and watching videos on my phone about homelessness, which only increased my anxiety. There's a stigma that homeless people are just drug addicts or criminals, but that's not the case. Most become homeless because they're already living in poverty or don't have access to affordable housing, which is sad.

Anyway, I even joked with my best friend about letting us camp out in her backyard if things got out of hand and I needed shelter, a place to go to the bathroom or bathe. At least I knew I had my best friend who wouldn't let us falter. I researched all my options just in case something like that happened to us, and I found out that there were churches and food banks available. It's important to always know your resources in a sticky situation. Some homeless people live out of their vehicles, but that's no way to live either. You're cramped in a small space with nowhere to store your belongings, and there's no bathroom.

I've given to the homeless before. One man in Newport News stood holding a sign at the beginning of Warwick Blvd after getting off the James River Bridge. He told me that he and his wife were homeless and that he was studying to be a pastor at his church. All he said was that he was grateful to be alive and that God is faithful. He's right—the Lord is always faithful.

Growing up, I was a bit naive. I had no idea that homeless people existed. I never volunteered for causes like the Salvation Army ringing their bells for donations. My mom worked hard but never mentioned subjects like these, so I had no clue. The reason I care so much about helping the homeless is because of my late Aunt Arden. Her last job was with Virginia Supportive Housing, and her role was to obtain donors to help re-home the homeless and get them back on their feet.

On the other hand, my husband Bobby grew up in a different neck of the woods. He was raised in Portsmouth, in Craddock, which was considered a rough area. Bobby's father abandoned him at a young age. His mom and dad split, but his dad decided not to stay in the picture. It's a shame. His mom was left with four children to take care of by herself, which sounds very familiar—a lot like what my grandmother went through. My father, too, was abandoned at an early age. When the devil creates schemes like this in children's lives, it creates emotional problems. It makes the child believe they are unwanted and unloved.

It makes them question, "Why? Why didn't they want to stay? Am I to blame? Why didn't they love me?"

It creates issues on so many levels. Thankfully, Bobby was taken to church as a child by neighbors who lived nearby, and he learned early on that his true Father was in heaven and to rely on Him for guidance and strength. As for my father, he knew about God but didn't really seek Him. It was the '70s, and he turned to partying, cannabis, and alcohol—sex, drugs, and rock & roll. A lot of Christians believe this era was the work of Satan, with too many teenagers being irresponsible, going out, having unprotected sex, dancing provocatively, and getting into drugs that led to harder substances. Sin was on the rise.

JANUARY 2022

I was working at a popular local mattress retailer, and my depression had subsided. The suicidal thoughts had gone away since I had switched jobs, which was a good thing. Christmas had come and gone quickly; I didn't really want to celebrate it because I wasn't in the spirit. Then, no sooner had the new year come I came down with COVID. Lucas had strep throat and COVID-19 at the same time, but he bounced back quickly with the help of antibiotics. I think the strep throat affected him more than COVID did. However, COVID-19 caused me to develop pneumonia.

I was upstairs in my room, coughing and staying away from everyone else in the house. My mom kept telling me to go to the emergency room because she thought I had pneumonia. At first, I didn't believe her, but she asked if I felt a tightness in my chest and had trouble breathing, and I responded with a "yeah." So, I went to the ER. Sure enough, I had developed pneumonia. I was out of work for two weeks and felt very weak. I was taking a combination of Mucinex, antibiotics, and zinc, using an inhaler, drinking plenty of water, and resting in bed. Whenever I had to come downstairs, I'd wear a mask.

Even though I was sick, Bobby had been out of work since the summer of 2020, and we never got disability from the state, even with the help of a lawyer. Since it was during COVID, the judge couldn't physically see Bobby or his limitations and didn't believe he was disabled enough, so he was denied three times.

Bobby doesn't have half of his pelvic bone or his right hip bone, and he walks with a cane! He can only walk short distances and stand for brief periods. Not disabled enough? What a crock!

SPIRITUAL GIFT'S

When I first met Bobby, I instantly felt this magical, strong connection between us. There was something special about him—I felt it in my soul right away, though I couldn't quite pinpoint it. After weeks of getting to know one another, he started telling me about his demonic dreams and how he would battle demons in them. He would also talk about seeing strange things in the sky, like demonic faces. People had called him crazy or weird in the past, but I just accepted him, loved him, and tried my best to understand, even when I didn't.

Bobby began having vivid or lucid dreams when he was about ten years old, and in these dreams, he would be battling demons. As he got older, during his teenage years or early twenties, he also had paranormal or spiritual encounters. I know he's not the only person in the world to have experienced the spiritual realm—there are plenty of people with similar stories. However, in 2011/2012, he began to acquire what he called a gift. He told me he felt like God had lifted the veil from his eyes, allowing him to see the spiritual realm. He started seeing faces in the sky, strange objects, and even UFOs.

Bobby can see things that most others cannot. He first began taking photos with his cellphone but later bought a Nikon P900 and now uses certain software to manipulate the images. With special lighting, you can see things differently. He's shown me many of his images, and I can even testify that there are evil-like faces in the sky, dragon-like figures, and other strange objects. It reminds me of Harry Potter when the sky darkened and something ominous was brewing—like when they knew Voldemort and the Death Eaters were on the rise. The sky filled with dark, evil images, and when the Death Eaters were called, you could see the Dark Mark.

EASTER 2022 My anointing

This Easter Sunday was like no other, and I will never forget it as long as I live. I had a divine spiritual experience. Others, such as doctors, might call it psychosis or say my brain snapped with euphoria. But I don't believe that was the case, and the reason why is because it happened on Easter. I truly believe an angel, or the Holy Ghost, visited me that morning because I had decided to attend the sunrise service to worship. I don't recall feeling any fear at all. Prior to the service, the Holy Ghost instructed me to anoint my head, the palms of my hands, and my feet with frankincense oil. So, I did. I remember feeling an out-of-body experience, with a glowing essence radiating from my body that morning. I felt an overwhelming sense of joy and happiness from head to toe. When I went to worship, the sunrise was breathtaking! I felt Jesus's presence. I knew He was with me, as He always has been.

Ever since Bobby and I have been together, we have periodically noticed the numbers 2:12 and 3:16. These numbers, of course, mean something to us. The number 2:12 is considered angelic, and whenever I see 3:16, I think of John 3:16. I've watched Joyce Meyer's ministries speak about anointings, so I know they are real, even if someone else might call me crazy. I know what I felt that day, and it was very real. Why would the Holy Ghost direct me to anoint my head, hands, and feet with ancient oil otherwise? It wasn't the oil itself that made me anointed—it was the Spirit. God has given me a divine mission in my life and marked me to carry out His will for His kingdom. I believe everyone has the power to be anointed in Christ, but first, it requires accepting Christ as your Lord and Savior in repentance for your sins. Then, it requires getting to know God through His word and prayer. Chris Vahe explained the concept of anointing to me more clearly: anointing is the power of God upon a person to enable them to fulfill their divine purpose. It is the empowering force of God that enables a man or woman to carry out their assignment.

1 Corinthians 1:21-22 says: "And it is God who establishes us with you in Christ, and has anointed us, and who has also put his seal on us and given us his Spirit in our hearts as a guarantee."

When I reflect on my anointing and others who have been called to serve, I think of For King and Country's song "Broken Halos." Especially the part of the song that goes:

Busy breaking down the walls
Just to build defenses
Try to see the other side
But no one's bending
Way too shy to bare our souls
So, we shout opinions
But nobody listens

For Heaven's sake, we're missing hope
Been saving face and throwing stones, so
Take your mistakes, just let 'em go
'Cause don't we all wear those
Broken halos?

I think of this song because we all have souls and light in us. It's our choice to use it or not, to use the fruit of the Spirit. Most of us have broken halos because we are dealing with pride, sin, unforgiveness, and strongholds, and these things are keeping us from all of God's gifts and the good things He has in store for us. Referring to Joyce Meyer, she speaks about how many people hinder their anointing based on the mere fact of mistreating the Lord's children. Everyone is constantly judging others, being hateful, gossiping, saying ugly words to one another, not forgiving each other, etc.

Matthew 22:36-39 says, "Teacher, which is the greatest commandment in the Law?" And he said to him, "You shall love the Lord your God with all your heart and with all your soul and with all your mind. This is the great and first commandment. And a second is like it: you shall love your neighbor as yourself."

DEMONS IN THE BIBLE

They are organized under Satan in hierarchical levels known as rulers, authorities, powers, and spiritual forces of evil (Ephesians 6:10-12).

What are demons, according to the Bible? Demons can refer to both the forces of evil in the world and the devil himself. Throughout scripture, we are continually warned to be wary of demonic forces trying to corrupt and influence us. While many of the demons we must be on guard against are external, the Bible also reminds us that we may harbor demons within our own psyche—ones we need to recognize and expel.

According to the Bible, demons are involved in various activities. They are organized under Satan in hierarchical levels known as rulers, authorities, powers, and spiritual forces of evil (Ephesians 6:10-12). Demons have the ability to "demonize" people. This is what the Bible identifies as being demon-possessed, although the exact phrase "demonic possession" is never actually used in Scripture. People can be demonized, which is another term for demonic possession (Luke 8:30).

Many believe that about one-third of the angels joined Satan in rebellion against God Almighty. These fallen angels are what the Bible refers to as demons. Although the Bible never explicitly states that the number was one-third, this has been speculated by many for a variety of reasons (Isaiah 14:12-15; 2 Peter 2:4-10).

Demons can also take shape, different forms, and be visible to humans (Job 4:15). They may be exorcised or driven out from a possessed person, but this can be dangerous if not followed by careful spiritual discipline. Without proper spiritual care, the person may become vulnerable to a worse demonic infestation (Matthew 12:45).

Demons work to confuse the truth by using lies and half-truths (1 John 4:4). Those who worship idols and pagan gods are actually worshipping and sacrificing to demons. Demons deceive people into worshipping them instead of God (1 Corinthians 10:20-21).

The Bible even teaches that demons can inhabit animals (Matthew 8:31). During the time of the great tribulation, demons—who since the fall have been imprisoned in the lowest level of hell—will be released to wreak incredible pain and torture upon those who are not Christians (2 Peter 2:4-5, Revelation 9:1-7). Eventually, these demons, along with Satan, will be chained in the lowest level of hell, often called the "Abyss," where they will be tortured for eternity (Revelation 20:10).

Thankfully, God has given us every tool we need to stand against Satan and win. The best weapon we have in consistently defeating Satan is effective and constant discipleship.

MANIC 2022

This summer, I spent a lot of time at home. I was waking up super early thanks to my pink drink mix from the wellness company I was promoting! Every morning, I'd get up, start dancing, and praise God right in my kitchen, listening to For King & Country's "Amen." After all, the Bible speaks about dancing, singing, and praising the Lord, so that's exactly how I wanted to spend my time! I was also fasting, praying, and even doing my own holy communion at home. I'd pour a small amount of red wine into a cup, break bread, say the words of the Last Supper, and thank Jesus for sacrificing Himself on the cross for the remission of my sins.

On the other hand, I was getting a little out of control with some of my spiritual practices. I started buying sage and smudging outside the house to keep bad spirits from entering. I also burned palo santo and inhaled it, believing it would cleanse my soul of any unclean spirits. I even began consulting with a tarot card reader online, who convinced me that God had given me a spiritual key to a big white house I'd been eyeing in Franklin on Clay Street. I had contacted the real estate agent and gone to look at it. When I stepped inside, I felt spiritually connected to the place; it had everything I'd ever dreamed of in a home. I truly believed someone was going to give us the house. Somehow, some way, I thought someone would purchase it for us. I was so convinced that I even told my best friend, Brooke, that I was going to be her neighbor and live just down the street from her.

Then, things took a delusional turn. I started mixing fantasy with reality. I guess I had been watching too much Harry Potter, lol. I actually began to believe that other magical realms existed and that Bobby, Lucas, and I were really going to Hogwarts for Halloween. I thought someone would come to get us, and we'd apparate through a portal. My mind was racing—I even demanded that my mom hand over Bobby's disability money, about $9,000—and I blew through it buying all sorts of things. I even lied to a credit card company about how much money I made and ended up racking up $11,000 in debt.

What did I spend it on? Well, since I was mixing fantasy with reality, I spent it on stones—amethysts, citrine, carnelian, tourmaline, etc.—

because I believed they had special powers. And I truly believed it, too, because there are books claiming they have special healing properties and spiritual abilities. I would even stare at the stones like Gollum from Lord of the Rings, pining over them, captivated. The moonstone, in particular, felt magical—I could swear I saw things in it; my imagination was running wild.

I also spent money on a sales funnel that I never ended up using, and I invested in a nutritional program. At the same time, I had this idea that I was going to go back to college. I applied to Maryland's Master's Program for Clinical Herbal Medicine, thinking I was going to become a famous holistic doctor. My mind was all over the place, and I was starting to scare my friends and family. Even though the wellness drink I was promoting was safe to consume, I was taking in way too much caffeine, which started to affect me negatively. I was irritable, jumpy, and my moods were terrible. I was even getting aggressive. Something was clearly wrong.

To sell my wellness products, I reached out to an old guy friend on Facebook, and things went overboard. I met him in a parking lot, ranting about all sorts of delusional ideas. He listened. I was overly flirtatious and showed him the products, but my mind wasn't clear at all, and I ended up taking things too far, performing what's considered third base for him. I went home, knowing I had done something wrong. The next day, Bobby confronted me about it, and I confessed. He was furious. He shoved me hard onto the floor, bruising and swelling my shoulder. I didn't cry. Instead, I demanded his phone and threatened to call the cops.

At this point, I was given a timeframe to find a job, since I hadn't been working after getting fired and had only been promoting my wellness products. I eventually started working for a small Italian restaurant owned by a local businessman. But I continued behaving erratically and doing bizarre things. It was getting out of hand. I even invited some of my African friends to come to live with us in this non-existent house I believed we owned, and that's when things really hit the fan!

HOSPITALIZATION DIARIES

8/15/2022

I was picked up by officers at home before I could take a shower and finish business and work for the day. I was handcuffed for the first time in my entire life. When I reached the hospital, they informed me why I was there. I was not worried. I believed it to be my mother, Sharon Rose, who did it, but I was quite shocked when I found out it was my own husband who ordered an emergency custody order. I spent 72 hours (about three days) in handcuffs, cuffed to the bed by police authority. Every time I needed to tinkle, they had to unlock my cuffs so I could go to the restroom.

While being here in the hospital, I did my best to remain calm and just prayed. I requested the Holy Bible and was simply polite, doing my best to cooperate. Some of the police officers were a better service than the nurses, but I'm sure they were busy assisting other patients. Watching *The 7 Little Johnstons* on TLC, seeing their lives, and past episodes of their holidays and the Mother's Day episode was a delight! They gave me laughter and great joy while I just lay here strapped to my bed. One officer understood, exemplified great servitude, and treated me like royalty. We walked laps around the E.R. and traded a few waiter stories, though not as many as I would have liked because he had paperwork to attend to.

8/17/2022

I finally got to shower after two days of being here! My hearing was around noon. They decided I needed treatment for ten days, and I'm still not sure if they're keeping me here or transferring me elsewhere. It's pretty unnerving not knowing what's going on, but I'm just sitting here, hoping I have visitors later or that someone will want to come see me. I've requested my two best friends, besides my husband—who I confide in—to visit. Now, I'm just waiting, trying to be patient. Finally, I was able to make a couple of phone calls to my family since my cell and computer are at home, out of my hands.

Right now, I'm watching Guy Fieri's show, where chefs are competing based on quickness, accuracy, taste—basically everything. It's really intriguing to watch! I can only dream of the fun and excitement of being in a tournament like that. I mean, that's a lot of pressure, creating something exquisite in such a short time with so many rules and limitations.

My favorite nurse so far, the one who loves bandanas like me, saw me talking in the halls. She used her imaginary fishing rod to reel me back into room 4, lol. She said, "If you're going to be in the halls, you've got to wear your mask!" So, I hopped back into my bed.

Whilst being in the E.R., waiting to know if I was going to stay here or be transferred, I saw a lot in the hospital. I observed everything. I did what I needed to do to survive, and I know I will endure! One thing I've been trying to do is take short walks around the halls—this whole sitting still thing just isn't for me. After all, I'm a lot like the Energizer bunny, and now I'm back to a snail's pace!

Well, I'm currently watching the quartet of comedy—the funniest guys ever! Impractical Jokers is on. My cousin had the pleasure of meeting them a while back when they came to Virginia. I'm sitting here, snorting out loud, hearing them talk about that joke in front of a wishing well. One of them said to a stranger, "I wish I had less booty and more badonkadonk!"

It's moments like this, when you're just still that you realize who your true family and friends are. I thank God for these people, and I pray for help in forgiving everyone else.

Back to Guy—Guy's Grocery Games. It's been a long afternoon, calling family and friends, trying to beg for visits. I told them I was here—they all knew I was here! What's taking them so long to come to see me? Why should I even have to beg?

Fruit—I've always been more of a fruit bat than a veggie eater. Naturally, I'm a carnivore and favor meat and cheese the most. But this episode had me mouthwatering just from watching it.

After all, I'm just the girl from Virginia who never got to go to culinary school.

Still here, simply watching the Food Network. Nom, nom, nom! Oh my God! Heavens to Betsy, something to live for!

8/18/2022

Thursday, a.m. I'm greeting the nurses with good mornings, and they're being as kind as possible, telling me to go back to my room like the sweet, small moms they are. My laughter continues.

One of the best episodes of *Grey's Anatomy* was on Lifetime. I love that show—I binge-watched the entire series a few years back. I'd already eaten a banana, some nuts, chocolate, and some protein. Instead of focusing on what I can't do while I'm stuck here, I'm focusing on the good—on what I *can* do and what I'm capable of. And I'm capable of quite a lot! I've already learned more scripture and discovered the Australian scribbly eucalyptus tree and how a tiny wasp produces a special substance from the oak tree. Wow, who knew! It reminded me a little of the murder hornets created to torment others in *The Hunger Games.*

Another kind doctor appeared on the telehealth screen to talk to me about my so-called "manic" mind. I told him I knew exactly who I was, thanked him for his concerns, and said I'd be happy to consult with other therapists. He claimed I was out of control—that my energy, self-drive, and work ethic had scared the whole world around me. I'll admit that I'm a work in progress, and yes, there are areas in my life that need more order and control. But I won't back down from who I truly am in Christ Jesus.

And shame on me, I just looked at the clock again... Tik Tok, Tik Tok, Tik Tok. Man, how I miss getting on TikTok and hearing our little boy say, "Mom, let me see your TikTok video!" Lucas really enjoyed them and thought they were funny and cool. I miss his sweet face and nature so much. I know he misses me, too. Even though I'm not there physically, my heart and soul are with him.

Here's some perspective for everyone: sometimes, when people only see what's on the surface, they get scared. But look deeper—take a dive! Sink or swim—just make sure you see the bigger picture!

Thursday Afternoon

Hope on Thursday! Nurses are truly special—there are a lot of amazing ones here at the hospital. One got me a pillow because I asked, but she also joked, "No more yelling on the phone because Hong Kong heard you!" I assured her that Hong Kong was a *long* way off to hear me, but I've made some sweet Asian American friends lately! One even asked about my taste in watches.

The nurses watched as I did some plank exercises and abdominal crunches, and then I told them, "Hey, I'm running out of paper, ladies!" Thankfully, I got my wish for some morning java, and one of the nurses printed out some word searches for me to help pass the time.

Then again, you find yourself praying for people you've never met just because they're on your mind and heart. Let's just say I have a huge heart! I may be short, but my heart is **enormous**! Oh, how I miss working out with the Backstreet Boys, V.I.C.'s "Wobble," and J. Dash's "Wop!" And I miss worshiping For King & Country—they're utterly amazing! My favorite songs by them are "Amen," "Shoulders," and "O God Forgive Us."

Thank God Bobby brought me some snacks to keep me from going hungry—waiting for hospital food is a real nuisance. Now, it's back to more *Grey's Anatomy* reruns.

Friday 8/19/2022

Now, I am not normally someone to grumble or complain! But Bloody Hell! It's Friday, and this place has allotted me just **one** shower! I am repulsed by this because I've grown accustomed to bathing 2-3 times daily due to exercising, bodily functions, and so on. The doctor came through on telehealth and wanted to know how I was sleeping and how I was doing. So, of course, I told the truth. I am stiff. Imagine going from sleeping on what's considered a luxury mattress to a hospital mattress that offers only a small amount of support.

Visitor: Kris. We went to high school together; we weren't really friends back then, but I was always kind to him, and he was always nice to me. We reconnected through Facebook, and we have way more in common than I ever imagined. We're both adrenaline junkies—we love rollercoasters and such. We've both gone skydiving, too! I was so grateful to have him visit me. He even brought me a meal, which was really nice. ◆ ─ ^ —

One shower so far while being in here… Then I think about how there's a drought, and some children in Mexico are lucky just to have clean water. Many of them have been getting sick because of contaminated water. I am grateful for this one shower; I truly am. But water—clean water to drink—is vital, folks! Be grateful for the smallest of things! Water is life. Jesus is life. No one can survive without water for more than three days. Sure, there are extreme survival tactics, but those are meant for dire situations.

Some things I overheard just outside my door were people speaking curses and illness over me and my room number. I immediately let them know who I am. There's a lot of misunderstanding in the world, and I used to be in that same place. It's because I believed all the lies that surrounded me, the lies about myself. But through it all, God has been faithful to me all these years. This year, I finally began to truly love and be true to myself.

Here I am, around 10 a.m., doing squats while watching Grey's Anatomy, and all I can think of is Candace Cameron Bure and For King & Country. It's do or die, folks! I choose God. I choose life. I choose joy. Jumping jacks, as suggested by another sweet nurse.

It's no secret that I've been promoting health and wellness for Fit Team Global since around April. I've been taking their amazing products since February—truly the best on the market! The products affect everyone differently, but always in the best way. For me, they've enhanced, increased, and accelerated my energy—my "bunny self," lol. I've always had a strong work ethic, always been kind to others, and genuinely wanted to help, even if it seemed over the top. With Fit Team, in a short time, my mentor Erin has shown me so much love. She's believed in me, cheered me on, shared in my frustrations—she's been watching and listening the whole time, like the big sister I never had. Erin is truly the best sister I've ever had. Just a few people can create the most powerful family and force, but it takes trust, faith, and belief.

I just received words of victory from Bobby, and it was pure joy to my ears! I was ecstatic—I even did a victory dance in the powder room, though my face had broken out from not keeping up with my beauty regimen. Bobby told me about the signs he's been seeing from God. He's starting to have eyes to see and ears to hear! Praise God! I kept telling him to do as I instructed and to remember: Obedience is better than sacrifice. This was his lesson, not mine. Even though I'm stuck in the hospital, I am still strong and useful. I continue to pray. I'm helping my husband from afar. I may not be beside him physically, but my heart and soul are with him.

Friday Continued…..

Thankfully, I have had another shower today. It is 3 pm, and I still have no answers about a better room or whether I am being transferred. I asked to speak with management or an administrator this morning. Suing has crossed my mind quite a lot. For a patient not to know anything about how long I am being held or what is going on — keeping information from me is completely absurd. For the love of God, I should have an answer by now! If I have to be here, then I need a better room and bed than what I have.

I am speaking with my nurse now about how I feel, and I'm just going to let it go for now and read the Bible. I even started to sing "Let It Go" from Frozen, lol.

Whew! Then, in the other room, someone was yelling and being irate. Not sure what was going on, but I had to protect my peace. It reminded me of my homie, Trent Shelton. He is such an amazing man of inspiration and motivational speech. My nurse was about to leave, but she brought me coffee since I didn't have my Fit, and the door was shut! I had my java and Jesus. Peace at last. Amen.

Shift change—new nurse—I like her. Everyone is entitled to have favorites. Likes, dislikes… I do my best to get along and love everyone, but there are just some folks who get your vibe better than others.

Well, I have made a few phone calls. Spoke my thoughts and requests. For now, I wait. Be still. This is something I need to learn more of being still, letting go, and letting God handle everything. He is in total control. Always. I found myself crying in Ecclesiastes and then holding myself and the Word close to my body while reading the Song of Solomon. Time here has done me well, and nothing is ever wasted.

My friend Kris just left not long ago. I was grateful for the salad he brought me. Laughter, talks, music… Harry Potter and the Order of the Phoenix was playing—and I was crying again at the words, "We have something worth fighting for." Well, I'll say it again: I am a huge Harry Potter nerd. Evil does not prevail! I have never been one for violence or hatred. However, if it is the right cause and the right type of fight, I am down. After all, prayer is your best weapon!

I went to brush my teeth and returned to my room. A little boy was in so much pain from a snake bite! I didn't know his name, but I just told him, "Be brave; you're going to be okay." I immediately began to pray for him. My heart broke knowing this sweet boy was in pain. I can only imagine. Dear Jesus!

Saturday 8-20-2022

I am waiting patiently to speak with the doctors so they can quiz me and ask their standard therapeutic questions. I know how to do therapy. I've taught myself over the years through all sorts of methods. I've already prayed and read the Word of God.

Now, my attention turns to a book I bought, one that teaches about nature's wonders. These two pages bring back memories from childhood—about cicadas. Oh, how I love the sound of them in the summertime. I can recall going on hunts for cicada shells on the trees where they had molted. I never saw live ones, just the shells. My childhood home was surrounded by woods.

As a child, I explored the woods often. It was a peaceful place. I would go into the woods by myself. Man, was I brave! Lol. It was a haven for me and many of the neighborhood kids. We even built forts and named small streams and such.

I was really looking forward to going to the local Pow Wow but never got the chance. I read scripture this morning and finally got some answers. But then the pain rushed in. I was told I wouldn't be seeing my little boy for a while because I was being transferred somewhere.

Knowing I wouldn't be able to plan or see my boy on his birthday made me sob like a baby. I ran to the bathroom to vomit. Pain can make you sick, too. But my hope is in the Lord, for I know all of this is being turned around for the greater good.

A commercial came on… "I love you, Drew. I always have." I smiled, remembering all the times Drew Barrymore made me smile, laugh, and feel warm inside just from her being who she is.

Speaking of Charlie's Angels, Cameron Diaz is related to me by marriage. My grandfather says she's connected to my grandmother's side through my late Aunt Mildred. She passed a few years ago.

Thank God my husband finally showed up with deodorant and some of my makeup! At least I could smell better and put on some eyebrows and mascara. I reminded him of his past and all the hell he had been through. I reminded him of mine, too. And then, I reminded him of all the hell we had been through *together.* That word.... "together," is powerful. We prayed together, we cried together. I pleaded with him to listen to the truth and not all the lies. He spoke with the nurses before leaving and kissed me gently on my forehead.

It's amazing what we can learn about ourselves when we have extra time to reflect and learn new things. Sometimes, when you least expect it, beauty comes simply from art. I don't know if anyone knows that I have always loved art. Since I was a little sea biscuit, I would color between the lines at my grandmother and grandfather's home! I would sit on the countertop around the holidays and take pride in my coloring.

God just reminded me of a special memory. He recalls it and reminds me that not everything we do is for the public eye. Some things we're meant to do behind the scenes. One thing I can assure you is that our Father in heaven sees your good works, and a good heart never goes unnoticed.

And another memory that God laid on my heart was the time I brought a meal to a special family in town. They were in desperate need of help after losing their 3-year-old baby girl in a traumatic accident. It broke my heart to hear their story. I don't recall what I made for them, but I just wanted them to know they were loved and my heart was with them. A certain someone scoffed at the time and judged me, blaming the family for the tragedy. My heart sank at this person's response, and I was disgusted. All I could think was, "Do you think this happened on purpose? Where is your compassion?"

Saturday Evening Continued......

My blood pressure was a bit elevated because I had some concerns, and I felt like a frightened little bunny, but the machine was super tight around my arm—it really hurt. We took it a second time, and it wasn't as high as the first take. I was informed of new information, and I was truly taken aback. All I wanted was for Bobby and my friends to be with me through this. But even in all the commotion, I remembered to open the most important book there is, and that's the Holy Bible. I don't care who you are, what culture or religion you belong to, your skin pigmentation, your background, or where you came from—the Holy Bible contains all the truth you will ever need. It teaches you everything you need to know and, most importantly, to love. God is love. "All You Need is Love" by The Beatles just popped into my mind. Since I have no cell service now, I can't listen to music, so I just sing and hum it from memory.

This has been the longest Saturday of my life. I tried calling Bobby several times, and no answer. He's usually good at answering. I even called my best friend, Brooke, one more time to see if she'd heard anything. I called his new place of employment—nothing. At that point, I knew this was in God's hands, out of my control. I cried and prayed some more. I'm trying to get warm because my emotions are all over the place. If anyone wants to understand, Bobby walks with a cane; he no longer has a right pelvic bone or hip joint and only one functioning kidney. I am worried. Why wouldn't I be? I tried to calm down, but I was hungry while watching Guy Fieri. All those delicious-looking dishes were so mouthwatering. Nom, nom, nom! Oh, how I wished for real comfort food, but for now, I had peanut butter, graham crackers, nuts, and sunflower seeds.

I kept calling to see if Bobby was safe—still nothing. This reminds me of the time not long ago when I was working at the grocery store. I had to stay late unexpectedly, and I wasn't home at my usual time. My family got a little frantic, and when you absolutely love someone, you can seem a little crazy to others around you.

Falling in love always puts us in that heightened emotional state— the first date, the first kiss, the first handhold. The sparkle in your eyes, gleaming back and forth at each other, the smiles and flirting. What do we call this? Hello! Romance! Romance has been around for centuries. God is love... and God created romance, too!

Bobby is, and can be, romantic. He asked me to marry him three times!

The first time was when we were a bit drunk and having a good time, but we were more serious than serious, even if we were inebriated. The second time was when he was sober. It was just as genuine; he had just come home from a long day at work, sweaty and dirty but still looking fine with his bronzed body! No ring, though. I had bought a ring set from Overstock.com with beautiful blue diamonds, something I'd always wanted, and I saved it in the box. The third time he asked me was the day our son was born. We made it official to our family, friends, and, of course, Facebook official.

Granted, we did things a little backward, like a lot of folks do these days. We conceived out of wedlock, which is still frowned upon by some individuals. But Bobby was already an amazing partner and daddy right away. He always brought me what I craved, knew what I wanted to eat without me saying a word, and rubbed my swollen feet every day without complaint. I had to wear flip-flops throughout my entire pregnancy. I didn't have morning sickness, but I did have what they call PUPPP—an exceedingly rare skin condition that affects some women during pregnancy. It was incredibly itchy. Bobby had to apply lotion on me, and he was always there. During my second trimester, Bobby did something remarkable. He prayed, placing his hands over my PUPPP and asking God to heal it and ease my pain. It didn't go away instantly, but within a few days, it disappeared. God had answered those prayers. They came from love and belief. Bobby and I had created life, a beautiful, wondrous miracle.

Granted, I didn't look my best after the C-section—I was sick from all the anesthesia, exhausted, loopy, and totally unfiltered. But love was present, and he didn't care because, to him, I was beautiful. I had helped make him a daddy. Lucas loves his daddy. I know he loves me too, but his dad is his best friend ever! Even though Lucas favors me, he still goes to his daddy first.

Sunday 8/21/2022

It is Sunday, the day of worship! I do not have YouTube to pull up or Spotify on my phone, so I just sing from memory the best that I can. And it's moments like this on Sunday morning that I say, "If I were to lose everything, God, I'd still have You with me in song, prayer, Your word, the air in my lungs, and my beating heart." Now, I was stuck in Room 6, and I could not go to a House of God. I do not like calling it church anymore, even though many call it that. Joel Osteen just so happened to be preaching exactly what I was going through. I was not shocked—I just smiled and rejoiced, lying there, knowing everything I knew because of my relationship with God.

Patience is something I have been learning all year. I have been patient all year. I still struggle with patience now as I am writing this. I have heard that anything worthwhile, or a great reward, is never easy! God is not going to plop a million dollars in your lap from the sky! He is not going to lose that weight for you! God is not a god of sloth and laziness! Now, I understand there are some folks out there who have ailments, disabilities, and other struggles that I am unaware of, but I can tell you that you are still of great use! Find out the things you can do, and let God take care of the rest! God knows of your struggles within your body! He will never leave you nor forsake you. If you cannot use your body, use your brain! If you cannot dance, use your voice instead! Quit making excuses!

When you know God, and He has truly revealed Himself to you, suddenly, you have no worries because He shows you the way! Another movie, one of my absolute favorites, came on television, and I was so happy because I knew it was meant for me to see. The Princess Diaries had just ended, and The Royal Engagement had just come on.

MY SECRET ANCESTRY

Well, I have a secret that only a few know that I just cannot hide any longer. It explains why my mother always said, "You have champagne taste on a beer budget!" (lol).

I am of royalty. My bloodline and lineage are phenomenal. I am tied to the royal family in the U.K., even though I am an American citizen. All my ancestors are of Greatness. I had my own family telling me it does not mean anything. Excuse me? Shut the Front Door! It means everything! It explains who I am and where I came from. It explains it all!

Who am I related to? DNA does not lie. I am related to Alfred "The Great," King of Wessex. He is my 31st great-grandfather. Our late Queen Elizabeth II of England is my 28th half-cousin 3x removed. God rest her soul.

***I owe my ancestry reports to the Lord and my late Aunt Arden Virginia Reed for leaving me those reports, always loving me, believing in me, and guiding me in the right direction. She was an amazing human being! I plan to honor her name and carry out her legacy. She was and is incredibly special to me.*

King Charles of England is my 20th cousin 1x removed, and Prince Henry "Harry" and Prince William are my 21st cousins. I'm related to Prince Edward, Duke of Kent, Queen Victoria of Great Britain, Edward VI, King of England, George VII, King of England, as well as George I & II, Kings of England. Aethelred II "the Unready," King of England, Edgar I "The Peaceful King" of England, Edmund I, King of England, Edmund II "Ironside," King of England, Edward I "Longshanks" Plantagenet of England, Edward I "The Elder," King of England, as well as Edward II, III, and VII. Also, King George III, V, VI. King Henry I, II, III.

I'm also related to Mary, Queen of Scots, and James I, II, III, IV & V, Kings of Scots.

As far as American history goes, my grandmother, Pansy Nadine Lee, whom I am named after, and my grandfather, Sidney Lee, are related to Robert E. Lee of the South; he is my 4th cousin 6x removed. William Lee was my 8th great-grandfather, Richard Henry Lee, my 7th great-grandfather, John Esquire Lee, my 6th great-grandfather, Edward Lee, my 5th great-grandfather, and Edward Lee Jr., my 4th great-grandfather.

There is so much more I need to find out from my ninety-four-year-old grandfather about my mother's side of the family's ancestry, but all that I do know is that my great-grandmother, my grandma's mom, was an immigrant from Belgium. My grandfather's family is from England, surname Preedy, and most of that side of the family came from Gloucester, England. Much to find out and still discover!!

BACK TO HOSPITALIZATION DIARIES

Sunday Afternoon, 8/21/2022

Yes, the power of prayer really does work! If anyone thinks otherwise, then you need to go back to the house of God because that is a place for sinners. OOOooh, I said it! (lol!) No, even those who are not in sin should still go to worship and be a good example to those around them!

I finally spoke to a doctor this afternoon who is quite intelligent and exceptional. He asked his questions, I shared some honest information, and we communicated efficiently. I was certain that a breakthrough was on the horizon! All I could do was praise God with song and tell the officer about the good news! Hallelujah was definitely in my vocabulary!

Well, I called a certain family member to let them know the good news—that I was getting out of here soon! The doctor who spoke with me today believed I truly didn't need to be here. He just needed to clarify some things with my husband. Anyway, this person seemed a little relieved but also angry. I could hear it in their voice. They were still in disbelief about everything right before their eyes or about the great things to come.

I'm sure everyone has heard the famous saying, "Teamwork makes the Dreamwork." I'm going to remind everyone again who Satan is—he is everything opposite of God. He only wants to steal, kill, and destroy! He uses his workers, demons, to influence people's minds and hearts to carry out his deeds. He doesn't want anyone to be joyous, healthy, happy, or communicative. He will do everything in his power to isolate you from loved ones and disconnect you from God.

So instead of doing your own thing on the weekend, go visit your family and friends, fellowship with one another. Talk with one another and ask how you can help, even if it seems minuscule. No violence! Talk things out, cry it out. There is no need for violence—we already have too much of that in the world. It is just pure ignorance. Why would you want to hurt someone you love? I mean, yes, the truth can hurt, and sometimes it needs to come out, but it doesn't need to come out in an unhealthy manner. I've always joked around with people: I'd ask, "Which version of the truth do you want? The sugar-coated version, intermediate, or the blunt, harsh truth?" Some people's demons cannot handle it.

I've been laughing all afternoon from watching the guys from Impractical Jokers—shaking the walls, filling the whole E.R. with amazing medicine. One lady said she had never seen the show. I highly suggested it to her (lol). Another nurse and I talked about the show and the guys. We both agreed that if someone couldn't laugh from watching these guys, then they may be severely constipated (lmao) and may have some serious mental health issues. I mean, they literally touch on every subject possible just for jokes and to make one another laugh.

I've also been watching Aladdin—the new live version. Will Smith and the whole cast are utterly amazing. They portrayed everything so well; they were all so talented and beautiful.

Sunday evening 8/21/22

Back to ancestry talk. We had begun the search for Bobby's ancestry, and it has been a mystery. We are still trying to figure it out. The only thing we know is that he has extraordinarily strong Native American and Nordic roots. It makes sense why he has always felt connected to seeing spirits in the sky. Yes, Bobby is quite the sky man! When others were calling him stupid and crazy his whole life, I saw a gift. I saw something in him. I have never understood him entirely, but I never called him crazy or stupid for the things he saw. I just didn't understand. It was God who brought our souls together. God heard our hearts and souls; He heard our quiet prayers.

Of course, my quiet prayers used to be in the shower or on my old kitchen floor when I felt hopeless like nothing would ever change. But it did, for the better. I used to be married before Bobby, and I prayed for that marriage and for that person, regardless of how I was being treated, because I genuinely loved them. But the Lord had different plans. God always knows what's best for us, even when we don't see it.

The problem with a lot of people is that no one trusts the Lord or hopes in the Lord. Trust your Father in heaven—He has you! This is no secret. Our God, Creator of all, is waiting on you!

Monday 8/22/22

So far, I woke up with a grateful heart and said my prayers. Today is a new day— to most, it's the beginning of the workweek. I poked my head out of the E.R., and it was quiet! No nurses around. I thought, *where is everybody?* Anyway, I asked a special guy nurse, *"Can I please take a shower?"* He obliged. Praise God! For the love of God, I got to bathe again! My fourth shower in seven days…yes, gross, right? I'm used to bathing three times a day. I went back to my room, laid down, and just turned the channel to REBA. Reba and Dolly together? Oh my Lanta!! I was laughing so hard, the officer outside heard me. I was bringing so much laughter into the E.R., the snorts were contagious! Lol. I try my best not to snort, but I just couldn't help myself. I even came close to choking from laughing so much, but thankfully, I had my big cup of H2O right by my side.

Then the lovely folks overseeing my case came in. Not sure if it was a judge or an attorney, but we all spoke, and it was recorded. Certain folks believed I needed further treatment. I assured them I didn't and that I was perfectly capable of making my own decisions. They said they'd contacted another nurse about some aid I needed. Today seemed to be going along perfectly!

My nurse for the day just came in and informed me that since I'd been refusing a certain drug they'd been trying to give me all week, they were going to have to give me a shot. I had no clue what was in that shot, of course. They don't tell you anything unless you ask. Then, I had a special visitor. We had never met before, but she listened to me and even shared her favorite song by Travis Tritt. She listened so attentively. She then explained that if I wasn't compliant in my case, if I didn't take my meds orally, I'd be restrained and given a shot instead.

So, I called Bobby to let him know what was going on. Told him because, honestly, he wasn't really listening to me before or trusting God—it's me sacrificing in here. So I prayed before taking the drugs they administered. One of the main side effects is drowsiness. Why do I need to be drowsy? I know how to relax all on my own. I know how to do therapeutic things for myself, all by myself. SMDH. I don't need this medicine. I only took it to make others happy, and I didn't want that shot either. I just wanted to go home. Trying to get everyone to see the truth around you is incredibly challenging. It makes me think of my love for M. Night Shyamalan's films—*Signs* with Mel Gibson, *The Village,* and especially Haley Joel Osment and Bruce Willis in *The Sixth Sense.* You only see what you want to see. How his mother accused him of weird things happening around him, like taking the pendant. The unbelief in someone—especially a child—when they're telling the truth, but you just don't want to believe it, or something keeps you from accepting it.

By being stuck here, I'm unable to contact my friends, my new friends in Africa. They've all been so delightful, and I'm grateful for every one of them. I've been talking to Bobby all afternoon, keeping him updated on everything that's been happening, but the phone keeps getting hung up on me almost every time. Whew! All I want is to see him.

Tuesday 8/23/2022

I was abruptly woken by a nurse coming in with a Covid test—they wanted to test me again. I said, *No. I am not sick.* As soon as she left, I prayed. My vitals were taken again, and everything was great, just as I expected. I asked the night nurse, who was about to go home, if she could stay a moment longer and quickly weigh me. Praise the Lord, at least I wasn't gaining any weight in here, despite being so sedentary. I can't burn fat just by lying around. What made me happy this morning was the simple pleasures: fresh water, coffee, and Jesus! Nothing else had changed yet. I was patiently waiting, being still. God knows all. I was really just waiting for the therapist or doctor to come in on the telehealth machine.

It's in moments like this that you wonder if you are on anyone's heart or mind—it's a hard thought to swallow. I hope the answer is yes. I had the TV on TLC again and was excited for tonight, if I was still here. At least the *7 Little Johnstons* would keep me company.

Then we played musical rooms in the E.R. We thought I'd be moving over to room 7 after being in 6 for days, but nope! Ha-ha. I'm staying in room 6. Well, back to thinking and reflecting—wanting to express gratitude but also recognizing how people, myself included, often take things and loved ones for granted.

Now, before you start judging, I've been guilty of this in the past too. After all, I'm not perfect—only our Creator God is, along with the Son of God.

You see, humanity gets caught up in the daily grind of life—work, chores, bills. Please, for the love of God, slow down and appreciate life! Enjoy your weekends with family and friends! If you've got all that PTO and vacation time, go on vacation! Stop making excuses and stop living in fear! It's okay to be smart and cautious, but don't live in so much fear that you fall into a rut, doing the same thing over and over like a rerun, or like a broken record playing the same scratched tune.

I can hear it now: *"Well, we don't have the money to go on vacation."* If there's a will, there's a way! Take out a loan, go have fun, and pay it back when you get home. That's what a loan is for. It's borrowed, for things you need or want to do. If you feel like the Scarecrow in *The Wizard of Oz* and think you don't have a brain, remember—you still have a heart, and everything else. Ask for help or advice from someone who might seem intimidating at first. They might just share some vital information with you.

THINGS WE TAKE FOR GRANTED

The simple thing is the fact that we woke up to start a new day! God allowed you another day, a new day to live—air to breathe and a heartbeat. The ability to see or hear—where some do not have this at all. Can you imagine? The ability to walk is a huge blessing! How blessed you are if you have two legs, and you can walk! Don't make me grab a frying pan and hit some heads! Just kidding.

Even though I am a lover and a Virginian, I'm in the middle of North and South but have always been more southern. Lol. It is in my blood. No offense to anyone. I have always enjoyed being from Suffolk, VA. It will always be my stomping grounds. It will always be my home here on this earth. I have spent a lot of time here, but something that I have taken for granted is that there are so many states and countries out there I would love to see and visit! How much beauty awaits me! This is what I mean about taking God's beauty and creations for granted and not appreciating them.

Thank God, Bobby brought me snacks last night! One of them is carrots! LMBO! Go figure.

That is a different story and book for my next one. I'm just grateful to have a healthy snack to munch on, though I wish I had some ranch to dip them in. Still, I'm just enjoying their crunchy, sweet taste. Carrots are rich in so many things—great for your eyesight.

Well, according to the doctor, I was doing much better within the last few days since we spoke. I informed him that I was doing my own therapy while being in here. He wanted to tell me that the medication I'm taking is helping me. How did it help? It was making me drowsy and sleepy.

Tuesday continued.....

Victory dance, no Covid! This day is getting more interesting. Apparently, my WBC is elevated for whatever reason. I could have developed a UTI or an infection from not receiving enough personal hygiene in here. Four showers in a nine-day period are gross. I have a sterile cup…waiting, lol…waiting for me to urinate.

While waiting—next door, there was some action going on. Violent, nasty behavior! I had already prayed for this individual. Anger and hatred were rattling the walls. I sunk down in my covers like a quiet little bunny, waiting for the right moment to dart to the bathroom. But I stayed in my burrow, lol. Meanwhile, I was watching Ashton Kutcher on TV on some show—this episode they were making a sandcastle.

I really do not like this medicine they are giving me. They are giving it to me at midday, and it is making me groggy and tired. All I want to do is sleep. It almost makes me feel like a lioness or tiger being tranquilized! Hahaha. Now that's making me think of the song *God's Not Dead,* "He's living on the inside, roaring like a lion! Roaring!" lol.

Today has been interesting, to say the least. No visitors, though. Thankfully, dinner was much better. I was grateful for a turkey wrap, a granola bar, chips, and fruit. Anyways, I called Bobby one more time before I settled in for the night.

8/24/2022 Wednesday

I have a whole new appreciation for local police officers. I had no idea how much nonsense they deal with daily. And the individual that was in the next room had many demons. Oh yes, I said it aloud. God has taught me how to know if someone has negative or unclean spirits within their soul. To drown out all his yelling, hatred, and cursing, I began to sing. Everyone in the E.R. heard. The charge nurse said, "You've been here this whole time, and we didn't know you could sing!" I've always been able to sing. I am a soprano, but I'm not the best with lyrics—I've always needed the words right in front of me. I'm already a writer. I even have a little jingle I created in my early 20s but never finished because I'm not a lyricist. I have the melody in my heart. I continued to pray for all the nurses. They need me here today, but I really want to go home too. I miss my family and friends.

Although it has been great learning about all the things medical professionals and officers do, it's not meant for the faint-hearted and the weak. They are all extraordinarily strong to deal with the craziness they face.

My new concern is school. I'm stuck here, and I'm about to begin my classes for my master's degree in clinical herbal medicine. It's my heart's desire to become a holistic doctor. I know it's a few years off, but I have goals for the future. Longevity runs in my family. I plan on being around for a long time! Both of my grandparents are in their early 90s and still doing well. Well, now that I'm writing this, I must tell you that my grandmother has passed away. She passed peacefully in her bed. Rest in peace, Grandmother Reed. Her name was Pansy Nadine Reed, maiden name was Lee.

I just spoke with my doctor, and they are talking about moving me up out of here, maybe to an actual room where I'll have more freedom. But this is not freedom. My freedom was stolen from me temporarily. I know who the real enemy is, and I have not allowed Satan to steal my joy or love for the Lord. I have been without my own clothes, no makeup, none of my food choices, no cell phone, no computer, no access to hop in my car and go to the store. When your freedom to do these things gets taken away, these are reminders of how we take things and people for granted.

Wednesday Afternoon

Do not lean on your own understanding. Sometimes God uses other people to show or teach us new things, and when we resist, we find ourselves in certain problems or sticky situations.

One thing I've learned about getting to know God more is that no one—absolutely no one—can hide or run from God. He sees and hears everything. He knows exactly what you're doing, where you are, all of it! Lol.

Some Phone Conversations...

Tough titties. Go sit in the corner. Anger. Bitterness. Stubbornness. I am not a beggar. Two phone calls. I requested to speak with the Chaplain because I wanted to speak with someone like-minded. They never came.

Mom came to visit, and at that time, two deputy sheriffs came to handcuff me and transfer me away, so she got to see me handcuffed. Danville was three hours away. I was being taken to a mental health hospital. When I arrived, I had to be checked in with admissions. It's a process. They check everything, they detect everything. I was asked how many tattoos I had. I was being stripped down. I put on my clothes—my sweats and garments that were assigned to me.

Thursday

I woke up in a mood of melancholy. I was a bit sad. I realized that I was here and there was nothing I could do except make the best of it and go along with the process. I missed Lucas. I even missed the one who put me in here. I knew it was not truly him. I have not forgotten who the real enemy is. I ate breakfast and went to the bathroom twice. Then I got to meet a sweet nurse from Nigeria. Something very comforting hit my heart. It makes me sad that I am unable to speak to all my new friends from West Africa. Not all my new friends are from Africa; some are in the States. I feel truly blessed to have so many new friends. They were all kindhearted and prayed for me, and I prayed in return.

10 a.m. rolled around. It is hard to pinpoint times of the day when you do not have a clock. Snack time. I was ecstatic to receive chocolate pudding, especially after learning about the cocoa plant and where it grows. Cocoa pods grow on trees and are normally red and strange-looking. It is the seeds inside of them that are roasted and eventually turned into chocolate. They are found in the southern parts of the Americas and West Africa. — ⌃ ⬝ ⌃ ◈

I got to shower. Hallelujah! And I got to call Bobby. He is such a heartthrob! We spoke briefly, for like 15 minutes. Lunch was good. Today is Thursday, and even though my heart is elsewhere, it is terrific.

I got to walk down to the rec room where the TV was. I watched the Wayan's brothers for a bit and chuckled. They were being good Samaritans to a homeless guy. Today has been terrific.

The food is better and healthier here, and I am getting treated great. They take mental health very seriously here, and I can say that I am overly impressed with this facility and staff.

I was just thinking about why I never watch the news. It's because it is filled with horror. Who wants to watch the news when every time you turn it on, something bad is happening? That's why I may be a little less informed about what's going on. The news can be so depressing!

We need to fill it with more positive and happy moments! Hope everyone can agree on this!

Friday 8/26/2022

It is around 6 a.m., and breakfast isn't for another hour. At least I had *REBA* on the Hallmark channel to help pass the time. It was my "Java" before the sunrise. Though, I really wanted some actual coffee right about now. I'm typically a 7-11 coffee type of chick, while my husband favors Wawa because of their specialty drinks. I'm proud of him for not waiting around for his disability money, especially since they said it could take years. Here I am, walking with a cane, working a good 30 hours a week. I told him he didn't need to work. But being stuck in here, I'm unable to do my jobs. Funny enough, my nurse practitioner here shares the same name as my husband's nurse practitioner at Duke Hospital.

Breakfast was sugary, and I have to admit I love a good combination of protein and sweetness! French toast is my absolute favorite! I'm a brunch type of gal. I wish I had someone to talk to... well, I found someone. Sometimes, you can meet amazing people in the most unlikely places. Almost like discovering a fossil that needed to be excavated—fossils are cool. They tell so much and reveal the whole story.

This medicine is making me feel dizzy, and the sugary breakfast didn't help—it made me feel sick, like I was about to faint. I got to speak with my uncle today, such a great and honorable man. He has taken excellent care of my grandmother and aunt over the years. I asked him not to tell my granny about where I am because I didn't want her to worry. Then, I spoke to an incredibly old and dear friend on the phone—she used to work for my mother.

Two of my close friends used to work for my mom. Hearing her angelic voice and encouraging words gave me peace. *The Mummy* with Brendan Frasier was the only thing appealing to me on TV this afternoon. I remember when all the originals were on the big screen. I was completely disgusted hearing how he was treated by so many folks for his weight gain and fading looks... I'm sure he's doing much better now. Before judging anyone, maybe consider they're going through something you know nothing about!

My stance on this—go to the source! Stop listening to all the gossip! Why don't you just man up and ask the person, "Hey, do you need help? Is everything okay?"

This medicine is making me sleep more, and it's also increasing my hunger. Before, when I was taking my product, I only ate when I was hungry, and it boosted my metabolism while burning fat. I really don't like this medicine; I could literally just take melatonin to calm down and sleep.

Overall, today has been a great day. I got to talk to the staff about God and Jesus, which made me happy. Then we discussed wisdom, psychology, and spiritual matters. I shared one of the gifts God has given me since I was young, and it has stayed with me all this time—the gift of forgiveness. If you can't forgive others, how can you expect your Father in heaven to forgive you?

8/27/2022 Saturday

Good morning, everyone! I feel great! I slept well last night! Breakfast was okay, but the morning shower was what really made me happy. I wonder what today will bring. It brought me contemporary Christian music and the realization that I want to sing and preach one day. I want to experience it so much. I know not everyone is going to get me or even like me, but I don't care. Truly. There's only one approval I care about now, and that's my Heavenly Father's approval!

It's funny how I'm stuck in the hospital without my phone, but my friends are helping me out, and I'm using a community-based payphone.

Today has been a day of prayer and spiritual warfare. Native drums... I came close to doing something, but my brother in Christ told me not to. He said God was already fighting on our behalf. It was quite interesting. I was planning to take action, but God assured me that two wrongs don't make a right, so I turned the other cheek again. I'll admit, I didn't want to turn the other cheek this time, but I did. I've been praying all day long. I've worked up quite an appetite, and I'm thirsty too. This afternoon, I doodled a bit. I drew a picture of flowers in a field with a rainbow, sun, and clouds for someone. I got to speak to a couple of friends today. Someone who was super kind gave me some chips and a 3 Musketeers bar, and it was fantastic! I was overjoyed to get a candy bar!

Sunday 8/28/2022

Want a ghetto espresso? Try mixing instant Folgers in 3 oz (about 88.72 ml) of water to get your caffeine fix! Lol. Now, I love Folgers—they're fantastic. Not downing them at all; they're one of the best coffee manufacturers around. I'm waiting for the shift nurses to come in so I can ask for the TV remote to listen to praise music this a.m. and worship. Since I can't worship anywhere else, this is it. Thank the Lord for Steve Furtick! I listened to his sermon about not worrying. *Do not be anxious about anything!* Philippians 4:6-8. His message was great! I laughed at his love handle reference and said "Amen" when he preached about starting before you see it. I listened intently as he talked about how we can either agree with the enemy, Satan, or with what God has to say about us. The choice is yours.

Sunday continued

I prayed for my enemies this morning. I really didn't want to, but I did it anyway—for myself, not them. See, I told you I'm not perfect. I didn't want to pray for them, but deep down, I knew it was the right thing to do. Lunch was good today—we had baked sweet potatoes, and they reminded me of Thanksgiving. I rested a lot today between lunch and dinner, mainly because I didn't have much to do. I got to speak to my special friend Chris Vahe from Africa. I can call him brother now, even though we have no blood relation. He is my brother in Christ. I'm incredibly happy we spoke this weekend—they've been very worried about me. Snacks have been a blessing. I'm enjoying graham crackers and peanut butter, along with chocolate pudding... Lol, *Forrest Gump* just popped into my head! Tom Hanks was outstanding in that film! One of his best! I first saw it at age ten but didn't understand it all because I was so young.

This afternoon was the absolute best! I called someone out on their B.S. in a nice, kind way. Then, I was a good Samaritan while stuck here in this institute. You see, even in sticky situations, you can still be of good use! The highlight of my week was eating a cheese sandwich and drinking Ensure while watching the MTV Awards. I was ecstatic! I was especially excited to see Taylor Swift's beautiful face on screen! Oh, how I loved her song *Willow*. Something about me—I've always loved willow and palm trees. Willows because of how romantic, sad, and lonesome they can be. Palms because they remind me of warm weather, Palm Sunday, and of course, Jesus.

Monday 8/29/2022

It's early, and I've had another "ghetto espresso"—lol. I showered and said my morning prayers. Now, I wait. "Be still and know that I am God" just came to my mind. This is entirely in God's hands. I had already spoken to one of my best friends today, and that made me feel joyous. I'm getting a lot of compliments on my tattoo here, which is nice. It's the Tree of Life—a willow and cherry blossoms, with a Roman clock in between, set to 3:16 for John 3:16. The most important verse in the Bible, in my opinion.

I hate being bored. I'm extremely creative and innovative, and being here is just boring.

Psalm 92 has become one of my favorites. This afternoon has been very sorrowful. I decided to write notes to Bobby and Lucas. Writing those beautiful notes made me cry like a baby. I hyperventilated. The nurse, with his "defect" jokes, helped calm me down and reminded me to breathe. He told me to take a hot shower to help relax. Psalm 13 and 18 have also been a comfort. Dinner is at 5 p.m., and I'm just sitting around waiting. The network is down, and there's nothing I can do. It's one of those out-of-control moments—it's out of my control.

Now, I'm listening to reggae in the sunlight, looking outside. The phone network is still down, and we can't talk to anyone! It's driving me absolutely bonkers!!

The night ended on a joyful note once we were finally able to use the phones and connect with loved ones and friends. After all, it had been out for almost ten hours! I guess they were working on the towers— who knows? I ate a lot of fruit and a tuna fish sandwich before bed, washing it down with ginger ale.

I woke up around 11 p.m., choking and coughing with the worst heartburn. Thankfully, the nurse heard me down the hall making awful gagging sounds. He gave me Mylanta. It was a rough night with broken sleep—I felt so bloated, and my stomach was all upset. Eventually, I went back to sleep until it was time for vitals.

Tuesday 8/30/2022

It's a.m., and breakfast came around. Cereal for the win! It was bland, so I added sugar. It's a morning of memories. I'm thinking back to when I was a baby. That's far back, but somehow, I can recall my earliest memory. I may have been 15 or 18 months old; I remember my Aunt Arden coming over to relieve my parents so they could probably go out to a party. I remember her trying to rock me in the living room rocking chair.

Continued

So, I was transferred to the other side. I was never sick with Covid. The facility was just taking precautionary measures—standard "Covid" protocol. Two "C" words are now like curse words to my ears, and that's Covid and Cancer. I'm only glad that there's more to do on this side, and I have more freedom. I hope Shelly comes back over here soon. At least she is sweet, and I can hold a conversation with her. I didn't have a pillow, so I requested one. Lunch was good. I ate and enjoyed every bite! I've tried to call Bobby and cannot get through. Times like this, family and friends mean everything. It's a shame no one has contacted me here. I know if Arden were alive, she'd be rallying up prayer groups and trying to get ahold of me daily! At least when I spoke to my uncle on the phone, he seemed to care, and they were praying.

Well, my meeting went well, I believe. I asked them when I can get out of here. They couldn't give me a straight answer, which was frustrating. So far, since I've been on the other side, I've been called the "B" word for no reason and was threatened to be punched in the face just for asking someone a question. I do not belong here! Thank God for the nurse I'm taking on a camping trip! For printing me out *What a Beautiful Name It Is*! At least I have some praise music to sing while I'm here.

Sometimes you can absolutely love someone, like absolutely love them, and not like them in the moment. I hung up the phone and waited for dinner. Then dinner arrived with gifts! It may be a small blessing, but I was grateful. Well, my sign from God came from, who knew!

Another devotional! This one just so happened to be Day 1 of *Be Still—Daily Encouragement for Moms*. It was about being safe and still. How did I know it was a sign from God? Because their son's name is Xavier. And our little Lucas's middle name is Xavier! It's also funny that the back of this devotional says, "Allow God to fill your cup." Well, I had just prayed for this before reading all my gifts. Answered prayers are always the best! But sometimes, they aren't always when we want them—most require patience. I spoke with one of my BFFs again… and it was medicine time. Time to settle in for the night!

Tuesday, 8/30/2022

I met someone nice. They seem very normal to me; they were just put in here to be evaluated and may have acted out due to anger or behavioral issues that weren't very positive. I already had one person tell me that I had helped them with trying to stay positive and not giving up, so that felt nice. So even if my time here is short, it's been useful. I went to the media room that afternoon and got to listen to some music. I listened to Bobby and my wedding song, *1000 Years* by Christina Perri, *Hallelujah* by Pentatonix, and *Shoulders*—my favorite by For King and Country.

Wednesday, 8/31/2022

It's almost 4 a.m., and I'm wide awake and reading. I cannot go back to sleep now. Too much commotion going on in the hallway. That's the thing about institutions—you've got other patients and staff making all kinds of noises throughout the day and night. Well, I didn't get the best sleep at all. Had someone hollering like an annoying sick rooster first thing in the morning—sounded like an alarm clock that was highly unwanted. I met up with a new friend, and we were already speaking this morning about various topics—very interesting American bloke! Then it was bloodwork time and then breakfast. I'm ready to do something and get some good news today. Well, the good news is that I got to speak to my doctor today, and that was about it.

Thursday 9/1/22022

Today has been a great day! This morning, I woke up early as I usually do. I've always been an early-to-rise, early-to-bed type of person. It's just part of what I like, and my biological clock naturally wakes me up.

I've had breakfast and made another ghetto espresso, lol—Foldger's did really help bring back some life to this decaffeinated coffee. So far, I went to two workshops—one on how songs relate to RECOVERY since that's the theme of September for the mental health institute, and one on stress management. I took notes just like a student would, trying to understand how stress and anxiety differ. I think I'm going to take a shower to pass the time before lunch. WHOOPIE! I got to play psychology bingo, which was a blast! I learned some psychology terms and a new definition in the process. I had a phone call with a good friend. They cleared the area, and everyone had to go to their rooms because there was a lockdown—someone was acting up and they had to put them in a straitjacket. I was really looking forward to my next class, which was on spiritual wellness. Oh! And I finally got reconnected with Bobby.

Friday 9/2/2022 – Lucas's birthday

Tik tok, tik tok, tik tok, I've been up since 3 o'clock! I cannot fall back asleep; my son was born on this day. I remember preparing for his arrival and being so nervous about the cesarean surgery. That was the first time I had ever been truly hospitalized. It's been quite a morning. Breakfast was okay; it wasn't very nutritional. I'm waiting to speak to Lucas this morning. I bawled like a baby—choked my tears back, but on the inside, my heart was breaking. I must have people pray for me today because I couldn't be with Lucas to celebrate his birthday. I spoke with my mom and some of my friends on the phone, which was nice. A couple of people shared items with me this afternoon. It was very sweet and made me feel special since I couldn't be with Lucas.

One of the guys, the one that's a jack of all trades, gave me some of his chocolate Rice Krispy treat. The point of today is this: even in darkness, happiness can be found if one remembers to turn on the light! My hope was to be home with my son for his birthday, and I even tried planning a party for him while being stuck in here, but they postponed it. I'm such a Harry Potter nerd. I connect with Harry on so many different levels. He is a brilliant character that J.K. Rowling created—he's just so relatable. Not just for me but for so many people. Makes me think about the song "RELATE" by For King and Country.

Saturday 9/3/2022

Well, it was another restless night, waking up at 3 a.m. I asked for some apples and a sleeping aid. It's difficult to get to sleep or stay asleep in a place like this. Breakfast was pretty good; we had muffins, cereal, and yogurt. I made another ghetto espresso again.

We had this new older woman admitted to the hospital. She was completely out of her mind and tried touching everyone. She even touched me—she touched my boobs!! I wasn't expecting that at all! I told her to get off me! We all laughed about it as a group in the hall and said it was better than watching TV, mean, but true.

I walked down the hall because someone was calling my name. I really felt like dancing for a bit. I love hip-hop—maybe because it's smooth, has a great rhythm, and is easier to dance to? One of the girls who is a resident here made my day by giving me some chips and cookies! Then I received a phone call from one of my good friends. Lindsay is extremely sweet and has such a beautiful, angelic voice—very calming and soothing! I loved talking to her because I always feel a certain peace hearing her voice. I love her! She is so talented with her singing and piano playing too!

In the afternoon, we all watched the movie *Push* and ate popcorn! Chris Evans is great, but I really enjoyed Dakota Fanning's acting—she's such a talented girl, even at such a young age. I especially loved her role as Jane in the *Twilight* saga!

Sunday 9/4/2022

Well, last night was better than the night before as far as sleep goes. I had to take more medication, some Tylenol—my menstrual cycle was happening again. It's been more irregular with all this medicine. All I can say is thank God for the Chaplain coming on Sundays to bring the message and worship with us! Today, my roommate Shelly came back from the Covid unit. I was grateful for her company. She brought chips, candy bars, and better soap! She also gave me some cards to send to my family. William La Cava had a phone call with his mom, who was a delight to speak to. She kept thanking me for being such a good friend to him here. At nighttime, it was just Shelly and me settling in our room, laughing about Winnie the Pooh and the Peanuts gang for some reason. I had a good conversation with Mom today; we talked about going to a painting night! I was extremely tired and went to bed early.

9/5/2022

It's 6 a.m., and William La Cava and I are awake while no one else is. We were already looking at the time at the nurse's stations. There was already too much action in the air—a green alert and then someone being rude as hell to one of the nurses, just because she was doing her job! I have already done my morning prayers and devotions. Since it's a holiday, groups were canceled, which sucked because it left all of us bored with nothing to do. I'm ready to go home!!!

We shot some hoops in the gym area and had some popsicles. My favorite movie came on—it brought back memories of the first time I saw that movie at my aunt's house. It's *The Breakfast Club*.

I love how they all just showed how REAL they were with one another, revealing their true selves. John Bender makes a good point... my legs and feet hurt from standing on the concrete floors. I had a phone call. Then the bathroom was dirty—there was poop everywhere! Thank God, someone cleaned it up quickly!

Tuesday 9/6/2022

So, breakfast came and went. La Cava really has me going with these comic impromptus. I've got about five so far; they're corny but funny... I spoke with my doctor about Bobby this morning, so hopefully that's happening. Now I'm in a class about integrated behavioral health, anger in all its forms, then comes stress management again. La Cava and I made a "Transformation Tuesday" and were collaborating pretty well on comic creativity. It was a day full of emotions, which ended well with spiritual wellness, hoops, etc.

Wednesday 9/7/2022

Well, so far, I got better sleep last night without needing a PRN. I had to sleep naked because it was so hot—the air conditioning in here sucked! It really doesn't work well in these tiny rooms; the circulation was terrible. Breakfast was decent, but I had to wait two hours in between for the next class, which was Tai Chi. It was fun, with a lot of slow movements for the body. Today, I spoke with the doctors about my situation, my status, getting some facts straight. Then I painted a birdhouse during craft time.

Thursday 9/8/2022

Thank you, *For King and Country*! I was singing the lyrics from *Shoulders* from memory, said my morning prayers, and read the living word of God. Today's scripture was from Hebrews 3:12-19. All I can say is that I hope my life and book will be a testimony to many and that it helps people. Chapter 3 speaks about unbelief and doubting God, which is another great evil! My doctor just came in and informed me they wanted to talk to me about something, but I had no idea what. I really hate anticipation. Waiting for answers is the worst, especially when you've already been patient. Patience... that word. That's the fruit of the Spirit! Well, today I found out that I have a mood disorder, or I am diagnosed with bipolar disorder. Thank God I'm not crazy! I knew that before coming here anyway.

TALENT SHOW!!! Comic comedy, overall an enjoyable day. I had to avoid a couple of individuals. We had brownies and fruit punch, and we all made tie-dye shirts outside.

Friday 9/9/2022

Today, I am in tears... I have been here way too long. They want me on another medication before I am discharged. I talked to my other best friend on the phone for a bit. Brooke has been a saving grace since I've been here, amongst other people. I called my father again for like the umpteenth time to tell him what was going on and that I loved him. I am really looking forward to coming home to my family, cooking, and cleaning again—I'm excited. I need to do something so bad. I had good conversations with Mom again today. Later that evening, Shelly and I were laughing because we had bad gas, and I stunk up my own cloud, lol!!! Shelly sprayed!

Saturday 9/10/2022

I am on a new medication. So far, I feel like my body and brain are getting used to it. It's made me very tired. I was worried about the first one they wanted to give me, but I requested an alternative. After all, it's my body. The ventilation here stinks, and I am sweating. I'm ready to take a cold shower—I feel gross. I asked if I could still take vitamins while on my medication, and it's perfectly fine. I called home, and my stepdad answered the phone. Bobby Ray is a great man—a man of few words, simple, but overall, a good Christian man. I told him I loved him before hanging up. Today has gone by so slowly. I don't know what to do with myself. It's just too slow.

9/11/2022

Chris Vahe from Africa called. He has become a loyal friend of mine. The first thing he said was, "Happy Sunday!"—which was nice! I talked to my mom briefly, and it was a polite conversation as usual. I took a nap. Twix for the win! Morale boost, for sure.

9/12/2022

Today is a special day—it's my brother's birthday. He was born on my grandmother's birthday! She got an extra special gift that year. And my devotional matches up with my story, lol! Today will be a good day!! I got to talk to Bobby on the phone...that made me happy!

9/13/2022

Today has been a great day. I didn't get the news I wanted, but overall, it was good. I have a cute intern following me around—he's in his junior year of nursing school. I finally got to go outside today! I cried. It was the first time I'd been outside in a whole month. Wow. Freedom. The things we take for granted. I received four bags of cookies for attending all my groups, but I wanted to give one away.

Wednesday, 9/14/2022

My left hand hurts bad from getting bloodwork done through it. I have tiny veins, and the nurses have difficulty finding them in my arm. Today, we have an ice-cream social and bingo—heck, it's something to do. The ice cream was great! We had sundaes, and it was a happy moment for a Wednesday.

Thursday, 9/15/2022

I had a weird dream that gave me anxiety when I woke up! As soon as I said my morning prayers, the anxiety went away. We can really work ourselves up badly if we let anxiety get the best of us. Today's courses include stress and anger management and mental health insights. I had my civil hearing today; it went very well. I plan to sell my gun because I have no business owning one. I'll never be able to own another firearm again. The doctor is upping my meds to get the therapeutic levels right. I just ate an entire Hershey's with Almonds bar and enjoyed every piece of it. I'm doing my best to stay awake during the day—it's difficult. Honestly, I feel like my book, which is a memoir, is the only thing I have now. I've been listening to some contemporary music and crying, thinking of my grandfather and about forgiveness. My life story and memoir are meant to glorify God! My memoir has been put on the backburner because it's a much larger project that requires more time. It's not the same story as this one. Brooke has been a saving grace for me, even if only for a few minutes here and there. I told Bobby that all I wanted was for him to hold me when I returned home.

Friday, 9/16/2022

This a.m. is my first morning waking up with more medication in my system. They're checking my therapeutic levels. Matthew, Chapter 6, has kept me going these past two days. It really helps to read the Word and pray. I spoke with my doctor today about adjusting my medication again, tweaking the times so I don't feel so sedated. I really hate that I need medication to function properly. I wish my brain produced enough serotonin and dopamine on its own, like it should.

Saturday, 9/17/2022

Well, so far so good—today, I feel pretty good! I feel a little better and not so groggy. But it seems like whenever I sit or lie down, I get sleepy. I really need to create energy by doing stuff. I miss coffee terribly; it's been over a month since I've had any real caffeine. Today was rather boring. We got to watch a movie, but it was all right—nothing extraordinary. It was a Redbox special, and honestly, I didn't think it had a very good plot.

Sunday, 9/18/2022

What does transformation look like to me now? Well, when I first began my transformation journey at the beginning of the year, it felt fabulous. I was worshipping in all kinds of ways, but I wasn't listening to my family or friends. What happened, according to the doctors, was that I was experiencing a manic episode without realizing it. I was in a high mania, and no drugs were involved. Thankfully, no one was hurt during my episode.

During my mania, I was mixing reality and fantasy together, and I became delusional. Truthfully, I know the difference between reality and fantasy, but it's funny how our brains work. We explained to our son that I had a "boo boo" in my brain and needed to be in the hospital to get better. When I first went elsewhere, I saw my mom as an enemy when, honestly, she was just trying to help me but didn't know how. I thought she was conspiring against me with my husband. Crazy, right? In my mind, it seemed that way—it was the mania, not me. So, transformation looks quite different to me now. Before, I felt I needed to look and feel a certain way. God has opened my heart to less judgment of myself. He's opened me up to more acceptance of love. I know now that there is help when I need it, and I need to practice self-care and good coping skills.

I am alive. I am grateful to be here. I have a mental illness because it runs in my family, and it's not my fault. I must learn to live the best I can with it. I love God and Jesus very much. When I get home, my story does not end. I'm not really going home—my true home is in heaven. Bobby picked me up from the hospital, and I was overjoyed. I gave him a huge hug and a huge kiss! He brought me a bunch of candy for the long ride home. All I wanted to do was get home and stay home. I missed Lucas.

RETURNING HOME FROM THE MENTAL HEALTH INSTITUTE

After returning home, I was not myself. I was very happy to be home, to see Lucas, and to be in my comfort zone, surrounded by familiar faces and loved ones. But I felt like a zombie—I was so overmedicated. Bobby had to assist me to the clinic down the street; I could barely walk. My body was in shock from the trauma of being hospitalized—it almost felt like jail and then being released. I couldn't even drive. I was afraid to leave the house. I had lost my job. My phone had been disconnected, along with the number I'd had for over 20 years, and that felt like losing a part of my identity.

My connection to social media was gone too. In a sense, I felt like Job, though we all know Job had it way worse. I had become a couch potato. My sweet friend Lindsay came to visit me after I got out of the hospital; she brought flowers, sweet treats, and such kind words. She was like an angel—her voice and her spirit always uplifted my soul.

I was swaying back and forth a lot; my mom noticed that I couldn't stay still. I was very fidgety. I had a difficult time relaxing, and my anxiety was still there. I was on the drugs Abilify and Depakote. At the mental health institute, bedtime was around 7:30 or 8:00 p.m.—basically right after meds. So, after I returned home, I felt compelled to keep the same routine and go to bed around the same time in the evenings. I couldn't help it, but then I would wake up super early, before the sun, with no one else awake and nothing to do, feeling so lonely.

Slowly, I began to drive again. I started with small trips, taking and picking Lucas up from school. That was about all I could manage, as the school was not far from home.

2023 - Attempting To Get Back To Normalcy

Since Bobby had already been working at **our** local gas station every day, he talked to the manager and helped me get a job. I had **slowly started** driving again, but I still didn't have a cell phone. So, I was only making small driving trips from home to and from Lucas's school, which was conveniently right down the road. However, every time I drove, my anxiety was still high. I felt nervous and afraid behind the wheel, and I think my **medication** had something to do with that feeling.

I began working the night shift at the gas station, and it was going alright. It wasn't a hard job, and staying awake in the middle of the night wasn't difficult. The most challenging part of working night shifts, though, was **sleeping** during the daytime—and believe me, it isn't for everyone. My **friend**, Brooke, warned me about working the night shift and said she didn't think it would be the best thing for me, given my mental health. She said it could really mess up your body's equilibrium. I convinced her that I'd be fine and that I didn't see another way to manage **who would take Lucas to school and pick him up**, so I felt like working nights was my only option.

I had informed my psychiatrist that my medicine was causing me to have bathroom accidents—and I'm not talking about pee; I'm talking about **#2** accidents. There were no warnings at all! One of Depakote's side effects is diarrhea or loose bowels, and it would hit me out of nowhere. I'd dash to the bathroom, but before I knew it, **it would already be running down my leg or in my panties!** It was disgusting and embarrassing. Why do medicines have to have such horrible side effects? When I saw my doctor next, I told her, **"You've got to get me off this stuff—now, please!"** So, we changed my medicine to Saphris, at a low dosage.

After a couple of months, Bobby got hired at a popular warehouse **that's now** one of the world's largest shipping industries, with warehouses all over the country. As soon as he got hired, I followed suit and applied for a job there as well. They were paying $16 an hour to start, which wasn't too bad—it was better than the gas station. I'd never worked in a warehouse before, but I figured **it's** a job! Once again, I chose to work the night shift, which was 6 p.m. until 6 a.m.— a 10-hour shift, four days a week. I worked Sunday, Monday, Tuesday, and Thursday and then had three days off.

One thing I liked was that we could wear our own clothes, and they supplied steel-toe shoes. They put me in a department upstairs called "Stow." It was okay, but I didn't like it—it was all sorting. You had to scan the items, put them in a bin, and let the robot bring you a new bin if the item didn't fit properly. After a couple of weeks, I got the chance to move downstairs to the receiving area, called "Decant." This job was much easier: I just had to open boxes, scan the items, place them in totes, and send them down the assembly line. But doing this kind of repetitive work for ten hours straight became tedious fast. I grew to loathe what I was doing. I loathed going to work, especially at night. There was no social interaction with my co-workers except on our two 30-minute breaks—one unpaid and one paid.

After being in Decant for about a week, a girl I'd gone to high school with recognized me. She said hello, told me her name, and I remembered her. I don't recall us having any classes together or mutual friends, but I did remember her.

After a couple of months of working in the warehouse, my mental state wasn't getting any better. At home, I tried to sleep during the day, but I wasn't sleeping well. I wasn't taking care of myself either; I still wasn't showering regularly. Bobby would tell me to take a shower because he could smell me when I stood near him, but I **just refused.** I didn't care. I was still very depressed, with lingering thoughts of hopelessness and anxiety. The devil had gotten ahold of my mental state again, and darkness had returned—not as strong as back in 2021, but still, a dark presence was attacking my mind.

Several nights at the warehouse, I'd find myself battling fears of homelessness. I worried that I'd have to give up Lucas to family members because I didn't think I could care for or provide for him. **Satan had me believing** that I might end up committing crimes to survive on the streets and go to prison, just to have food and shelter. I knew some people do that out of desperation because I'd read about it in my spare time, during those anxious nights.

Before work, I'd sometimes sit in front of the television, obsessing over articles on homelessness and prison life, convinced that this was my fate—that I'd never amount to anything. I felt worthless. I just sat there watching NASCAR, constantly glancing at the clock, dreading the fact that I had to go to work.

With summertime approaching, Lucas was going to be out of school, which meant he'd be awake in the mornings, and I'd get even less sleep during the day. Because I was working nights, I wasn't home in the evenings to take my medication at my usual time. Eventually, I just stopped taking it altogether without telling my mom or Bobby. Since I stopped taking my medication, my anxiety worsened. I was having a hard time relaxing, even at home. I wasn't motivated to do much of anything around the house. I did the dishes, and that was about all. Lucas and I shared a room, and it was a wreck. The bathroom was dirty. Bobby would plead with me to wash clothes—sometimes I'd comply, but other times I just wouldn't. My mental health was **not in a good place**. Brooke would talk to me on the phone, listening to me vent and share my worries. I'm so thankful to have her as a friend.

June

I got fired again from another place. Everyone around me was disappointed in me—I could tell. In a way, though, I felt relieved. I hated that job, and I hated working overnight. I knew I had to do something different. I became a couch potato again for a while. But by day two, I was already back to applying for jobs. My friend Brooke said she was proud of me for putting myself back out there right away and trying to get back on my feet again. So, I decided to go back to serving in restaurants, returning to what I know best.

Self-Care 101

I am a hypocrite, right?

Well, in a sense, we all are! Here I am about to explain the importance of self-care to you, and I have done the complete opposite! Please forgive me; I wasn't in the right frame of mind. I wasn't practicing self-care, and I surely wasn't loving myself or enjoying the things I was passionate about.

For the love of God! Take a shower! Even when you are in your lowest place and the devil has got you down, take a shower! Looking back now at me not bathing, I wasn't necessarily sulking. The devil and his workers had me believing that I had no self-worth or self-value. I had even given up on my passions and joys. I'll say it again: the devil comes to kill, steal, and destroy! He will use any tactic he sees fit in your life to attack and bring you down! He wants you to feel isolated and wants you to be disconnected from the Lord so he can keep you feeling worthless, helpless, and defeated. But that is not the case! We have a mighty and powerful God! He is the Alpha and Omega, and the Lord conquers all! Satan may win battles, but he will not win the war! This reminds me of Harry Potter again when Harry, Hermione, and Ron were walking with the others, and Harry said that we have

something Lord Voldemort doesn't have; we have something worth fighting for! Evil does not prevail! God is Love! Love always wins! Love is worth fighting for, always!

There are all types of self-care: mental, physical, emotional, social, spiritual, personal, environmental, financial, and work. They all can affect our lives in various ways when one or a few of them are out of balance. It is difficult to have everything in check all the time. I will tell you that all of them are very important and vital to living a happy life, but if I had to pick the top three, I would choose: mental, emotional, and spiritual. I'll tell you the reason why: it's because of the greatest commandment in the Holy Bible! In Matthew 22:37, "And he said to him, 'You shall love the Lord your God with all your heart and with all your soul and with all your mind.'" Our mental, emotional, and spiritual selves are connected, and if we are not focused on the Lord and staying in the word of God and in fervent prayer, then we can get unhealthy. We can get attacked by the enemy very easily! He will attack our minds and hearts first, and then it'll affect other areas of our lives.

Please, practice self-care and love yourself, whether it is going to counseling, talking to a friend, going to the gym, going to church on a weekly basis, meditating, walking in the park, treating yourself to a massage, listening to music, dancing, baking—the list could literally go on forever with ideas of various ways you can practice self-care! Just take the time to love yourself and spend time with loved ones, too!

Art Therapy

I have been painting off and on since I was nineteen years old. I took art classes in community college and thoroughly enjoyed them. A friend's mother introduced me to oil as a painting medium, and since then, I've mostly stuck with oils because they are the most forgiving of all paints, allowing for easy blending. Painting has always been a fun hobby for me and is also therapeutic, though I haven't made enough time to do it as often as I'd like. I've gotten a lot better over the years, but as with anything, improvement takes practice and skill. Practice makes perfect!

Art therapy has been proven to help people with anxiety and depression. It can truly help you unwind, relax, and take your mind off the everyday grind of life. I believe everyone has the potential to be creative. Our God is a Creator, and we are made in His image, so we can create and be creative in countless ways—and it doesn't necessarily have to be painting. Art comes in many forms.

August/September 2023

Prior to stopping my medication and my anxiety returning, I was still seeing my psychiatrist and counselor on a regular basis. I had confessed to my psychiatrist about quitting my medication, and she was disappointed in me. I just flat out told her that it wasn't working for me. I spoke up for myself and told her I felt like I needed something different and stronger. So, my psychiatrist put me on Seroquel, and then a generic version of it called Quetiapine. She said, "Let's see how you do with this medication, and we'll check back in six weeks to see how you're feeling."

After a couple of months on this new medicine, my brain began responding well to it. It was regulating my moods better, and my anxiety started to diminish. I started smiling again—and, heck, I even began to laugh again. I even started slowly listening to music again.

Christmas 2023

Christmas this year was so much better than in previous years because of everything we had been through. Plus, I was feeling like myself again. The old Sam was back. My personality was returning. This Christmas, I felt truly grateful and in the spirit of celebration.

Even though money was tight, we still managed to get gifts for everyone—all from Five Below. I mean, hey, Five Below is a cool store, with some neat items that are very reasonably priced. It's not about the cost of the gift; it's the thought that counts. Besides, Christmas can be overrated and a very stressful time for many people. But at its heart, it's a time for us to celebrate Jesus's birthday.

2024 - RECOVERY AND REDEMPTION YEAR

I am not perfect by any means; I am a sinner just like everyone else. I make mistakes just as everyone else does. That's why it's so important to confess or repent. But one thing I know for certain is that this year I am much better and more well-off than I have been in a long time. I have hope for the first time in a while. Hope—we all need that. It started off with me apologizing to my husband. Legitimately apologizing to him for my wrongdoings against him even though my actions were unintentional. My first apology said, "I listened to what you said yesterday. It was never my intention to hurt you or make you feel unloved. I'm sorry you married someone who has mental health issues. I never thought that would happen to me last year, but it did. A lot has transpired in our lives in three years' time, trauma. You do deserve to heal, and I'm sorry if I left you alone in that. It was never my intention to break your heart, if I did. Hearing you talk about leaving me recently breaks my heart, believe it or not. The things you've expressed really hurt me whether or not you meant for it to hurt me, it did. It makes me feel like you don't care about our vows to one another or our family. Like I said yesterday, you can't expect us to go from zero to 100 in the snap of a finger. For us to rebuild anything, it must start with forgiveness, which I'm sure you are struggling with, but you expect me to forgive you so easily...and please don't tell me that you're sorry unless you really mean it."

In a second apology I wrote, "No, I never left you like the other guy's wife did. In that situation, she was selfish and literally cast her husband aside. However, in our circumstances, I stayed by your side but in a way, I did abandon you. I abandoned you emotionally, and it pains me now knowing that I wasn't there for you like I should have been. I should have been more encouraging and supportive towards you in your healing, but I was not mentally there. I was consumed with my own depression. I am truly sorry for not being there for you. I am truly sorry for touching another guy's genitals; I sincerely was not right in my mind. It's taken a while, but I am communicating better and showing emotion again; I do feel better and more like my old self. I love you very much, and I do care about you and what you've communicated to me. I just hope you can understand and forgive me.

Forgiveness. Something a lot of people struggle with. Without forgiveness, healing simply cannot take place; it is meant to bring peace within us and bring peace and healing to restore our relationships. It is so important to forgive others because the Lord cannot forgive us if we cannot forgive others of their trespasses.

Ephesians 6:12 says:

"For we wrestle not against flesh and blood, but against principalities, against **powers, against the rulers of the darkness of this world, against spiritual** *wickedness in high places."*

Someone who has unclean spirits within them or is a toxic individual may be dealing with demonic forces they are unaware of carrying and act out towards their loved ones in anger, saying and doing awful things. You see, we are not dealing with that person but instead with their demons. No, we cannot always see demons, but they are all around carrying out the devil's schemes.

One depiction of demons that I can think of is J.K. Rowling's dementors. The dementors are soulless creatures among the foulest on Earth. Sound familiar? Sounds demonic, right?

They suck and drain every ounce of peace, hope, and happiness out of humans—every happy memory—and you'll be left with your worst memories and a sense of emptiness. I recall the train scene when the dementors boarded in *The Prisoner of Azkaban*, and everything went dark and cold, frostbite and all. They attacked Harry, and one dementor was sucking his soul. Ron, Hermione, and Professor Lupin were so close by, and thankfully Professor Lupin sent the dementor away before it took Harry's whole soul. I remember the line where Ron said, "I thought it was like I would never be cheerful again!"

You see, demons do not like cheerful hearts or joy; they are a part of the work of the devil, and they come to destroy as well. They come to take away our joy, too.

This is the main reason I do not watch horror films because they cause nightmares. We are not supposed to speak evil, hear evil, or see evil.

It's not good for our eyes because our eyes are the gateway to our souls. You can tell a lot about someone just by looking into their eyes. Eye contact is vital when showing you love and respect someone; if someone cannot look you in the eyes, there usually is a problem!

I damaged my husband emotionally without knowing it. You see, we all have the power within us to heal or destroy the ones we love. Our words are not just words; they have powerful meaning behind them. So does our tone of voice, which is something I strongly need to work on. Sometimes my tone is sharp, short, and snarky. We're all like children on the inside with our inner childlike emotions and our egos. We all belong to God and are created in his image; we are children of the Lord and must seek him as his children. God knows what we need before we ask him. The Lord knows everything we are going to say and do before we do so; he knows the number of hairs on our heads, he is the alpha and omega, creator of all.

Protecting my peace

Thanks to my inspiration, Trent Shelton—whose new book I plan to purchase and read—I realized I had to protect my peace. Some people might not understand, but I had to do what was best for me. I just had to quit my job at a popular fast-food restaurant because it was simply too stressful. I love people and food and have no problem serving others or working in the restaurant industry. But when a place only gives you negative feedback on everything you're doing wrong every shift, and then tells you they want to see you succeed, well, that sounds like bull crap to me.

After I got written up because two customers apparently complained about me not being friendly enough—which isn't true because I'm respectful, friendly, and cordial towards everyone—I knew I'd reached my limit. They wrote me up for not "smiling" enough! Never in my life have I ever heard of such a thing. Completely absurd and ludicrous! That's when I knew it was time to throw in the towel. A company that claims to be a Christian company clearly needs Jesus for real! We all need Jesus!

It's funny how you listen to your favorite inspirational speakers, music artists, and friends, and how they all encourage you to be the best version of yourself. They push you to persevere, reach for the stars, chase your dreams, and never give up! Lately, I've been busting my butt, although to some, it looks like I'm doing absolutely nothing. They just see me on the phone, the computer, or driving around DoorDashing. They think I'm throwing perfectly good seeds into the wind, or that my seeds are being choked by weeds in the soil. But I refuse to believe that! My seeds are being planted in good soil daily because I have the Lord and good people who love me, backing me up! In due time, my flowers—my garden—will grow, and with the right fertilizer, it'll thrive! It reminds me of that little rhyme, *"Mary, Mary, quite contrary, how does your garden grow? With silver bells and cockleshells and pretty maidens all in a row!"* I must close my ears to the negative Nancy's and the what-ifs, because the devil isn't going to win! Satan doesn't win! I have no room for doubt; it's not in my vocabulary or my thoughts any longer. Period!

Bobby shared some good news today! He spoke with his urologist, and his penile pump surgery has been scheduled for mid-May. I hope everything works out well. This surgery is part of his redemption process—really, it's part of our redemption process. What was stolen from us and lost will be restored. It's been almost four years since we've connected intimately as husband and wife. Sure, we've shared certain acts, but it's not the same. Other than my mistake during my mania—the mistake that hurt Bobby—I have remained sexually celibate. During those dark moments of demonic attack on my mental health, sex wasn't even on my mind; my drive had faded away over the years. After it was taken from us, I learned to accept it and just dealt with it.

Today, Saturday, March 2nd, I had scheduled myself to DoorDash because I needed to make some money. I had to hustle, especially after quitting my other day job. While I've been busy writing this book and setting up other businesses, I still needed to hustle! While people were quietly sitting on their couches at home on a rainy Saturday morning, I was out working. Thankfully, DoorDash pays by time now because some people do not tip very well. People should understand that DoorDashers pay their own way for gas to drive around town delivering food—at least tip $5 or $6 to cover a couple of gallons of gas, for crying out loud! Sheesh! I'm sure anyone who DoorDashes can agree with me on that **one!**

3/3/2024 Lucas's Baptism

Well, today is a monumental day in our family and in Lucas's life! Lucas was baptized! He is seven and has accepted his baptism in the house of the Lord. He did exceptionally well in front of the congregation—he didn't wiggle or squirm, although I think he may have been a tad bit nervous! Bobby and I promised to bring him up and teach him in the ways of the Lord with God's help. We also promised to raise him with the love of Christ in our home. Our fellow church members, the body of Christ, promised to do the same and to help Lucas in his walk with the Christian faith as he continues to grow. I was grateful today that my son was able to be baptized. I knew my Aunt Arden was singing praises in heaven and looking down, rejoicing for him! I am sure she is very proud! A few of our family members were able to attend: Bobby's brother, Josh, and my mom's sister, Aunt Jeannie, and her husband. A couple of other family members were sick or had other obligations that kept them from attending, so I just sent them photos. I really wanted to have a big party for Lucas afterward with food and a baptism cake, but we just didn't have the money.

Since I had quit my day job and was DoorDashing, funds were limited until I found something else. Even though I'm setting up a few businesses and working from home, it will take a bit of time before they're up and running, and time before I see any profits, so I need some other source of income.

Today, I made a bit of a scene at the park. I shouted at a young man to watch his language because there were kids around while he and his friends were skateboarding. I was talking with another mom there, and honestly, I didn't get the response I expected. Immediately, he snapped back, saying he was an adult and could do whatever the F he wanted to. He had a serious attitude problem! He started yelling at me and calling me the B-word, so of course, I replied and told him he didn't need to curse with young kids around. He kept yelling and cursing, and then the other mom got involved. He started arguing with her too. So, I felt like the best thing to do was to call the police. An officer showed up, talked to the young man, and then came over to speak with me. He explained that the young man and his friends said I had shouted at him first. I told the officer that there was some distance between us and that I only said, "Hey, could you please watch your language—there are kids around!" loud enough for him to hear me. But, of course, the officer said that if I'd approached him differently, like walking up to him, I might have gotten a different response. He also reminded me that since we were at a public park, the young man had the right by the First Amendment to use profanity if he chose to do so. After that, Lucas and I left the skateboard area and walked toward the main playground.

While watching Lucas play on the slide, I shouted across the way for him to get down from climbing up the slide the wrong way. The last thing I needed was a trip to the E.R. for a broken bone! I was on my phone, chatting with my good friend from Nigeria, Chris Vahe, and Bobby. Both of them told me the same thing—that I should have left the police out of it and just walked away. Chris said, "It's Sunday, just leave him be and forgive him."

Later, I was texting Erin from NY about my little encounter at the park, and she agreed with me that this generation needed manners! This generation of kids—maybe not all, but most—have serious "potty" mouths! It made me think of *A Christmas Story*, when Ralphie was helping his dad with the car parts in the cold and dropped the most important screw, exclaiming, "Oh fudge!" But he didn't say "fudge"— he said the mother of all words, the F-bomb! His mom made him wash his mouth out with a bar of soap that evening! Why? To clean it out! Why do we clean our bodies? To remove dirt, sweat, and dead skin cells. Why do we clean our homes? To keep them organized and stress-free. Why do we clean our toilets? Why do we clean everything? Cleanliness is next to holiness!

I went ahead and sent Erin some scripture readings that speak about cursing and what the Lord says about it. James 3:8-10, Ephesians 4:29, Psalm 109:17, and Proverbs 18:21. Those are just a few passages; there are more verses in the Bible on the subject. I know I'm not perfect, and I've said cuss words before, but I do my best not to, and I try not to listen to music that has a lot of profanity either. My opinion about profanity is that with such a wide range of words in the English language, why not use much more interesting and sophisticated words? Profanity feels vulgar, and it sounds very foul; those words carry meaning, so why use them? Just like I've never understood why girlfriends or best friends call each other words like "Hey H** or B*d!" Why are you downgrading one another?

They say it's just a joke or they're joking around, but I just don't find that kind of thing very amusing.

Timo, Timo, Timo!

I met my good friend Timo Fakoson from Nigeria on Facebook back in 2022 when I was going through my manic episode, although he was unaware of what was going on with me, and of course, neither was I.

A few months ago, when I made the decision to return to social media after taking a year and a half hiatus, he welcomed me back with open arms! I remembered Timo! He left an impression. I remember us singing praise music together over video chats. He sent me photos of his shop, showing how he sold clothes and shoes, and that he also does computer repairs. Since January, things have been nice! I was so grateful to know how much I was missed by so many people on Facebook. I reconnected with people I thought I'd never speak to again. I felt this immense love from everyone. In a way, it was good that I was away for a while, but then again, it was not.

Let me explain.

It was good I was away because I was not myself; I was a zombie... unreachable. But then again, it was not a good thing either because I was closed off and isolated, so others who mattered couldn't reach me or contact me. What if they could have said something to me that could have made a difference? Well, their prayers and thoughts while I was away still helped because I got better and returned. Timo became a better friend to me this year than ever before. He has prayed for me, and I've prayed for him. We've shared stories and Bible verses. Bobby and my mom didn't understand why I had to be friends with people in Africa. I didn't care. They were skeptical. Timo made sure I was eating and sleeping well every day, checking to see how I was doing. It seemed that I might be one of his only friends. He explained to me how bad things were in his country. I was already struggling, but he was suffering worse than I was; he had gotten evicted from his apartment. He had to come up with $100 to pay the rent, but he didn't have it, so he had to sleep one night in an abandoned building. The only way I knew this was because he showed me a picture. I found a way to help him pay his rent. I didn't want to see my new friend go homeless. I didn't tell anyone I helped him either; they wouldn't understand. I just felt in my heart that if I could make a difference in one person's life with this small gesture, why not me?

Timo has never asked me for money because he is too prideful. But I told him if I was ever able to help him, I would but couldn't make any promises. I've sent him money a couple of times just so he could have something to eat because his shop got locked up by the government since he couldn't afford to pay the taxes, and it hasn't been reopened yet. I was having a rough day the other day, and he sent me a little note that said:

Dear Sam, "I hope this letter finds you well, though I sense you might be going through a challenging time. Remember, even in the darkest of moments, there's always a glimmer of hope waiting to shine through. You're stronger than you know, and you have the resilience to overcome whatever hurdles come your way. Take one step at a time, lean on those who care about you, and trust that everything will eventually fall into place. Keep faith in yourself, Sam. You've got this! With warm regards, Timo."

I have to say that through all my mental health challenges and the darkness that overtook me, the Lord has kept me alive and in His hands. He has given me great friends along the way to give me hope and encouragement, and I am so grateful for not just Timo but all of them!

March 15th - Today is Timo's birthday. All I could do was wish him a Happy Birthday, send him a GIF, write a Facebook post, and send him a voice clip singing Happy Birthday to him! I wanted to send him a little money so he could buy a cake, but I just didn't have the funds to do so.

Encouraging the community on group

There are loads of groups on Facebook to join; some you can join freely, and for others, you must be approved by an admin. This particular group is a suicide awareness community for people who are depressed, suicidal, or simply need help in general. I felt compelled to join because I have been there and can relate to the people submitting anonymous posts about how they are feeling. Most of these people are ashamed to reveal their true selves, which is sad.

Since joining the group, I have shared some inspirational memes, scripture, and my own personal experiences. I've commented on people's posts, and I've shared other inspirational speakers, including one of my favorites, Trent Shelton.

Proud of Bobby

At first, Bobby was planning to go back to school for cybersecurity because there is such a high demand for jobs in that field. However, the classes were full, so he decided to take advantage of his company's college assistance program to pursue some type of certification that will help provide for our family and allow him to work from home, which will also be easier on his body. I am so proud of how far he has come!

He went from having to turn down his scholarship/grant for CDL school to being out of work for two years and not able to walk for six months, to learning how to walk again, learning how to garden, doing DoorDash, and eventually going back to work after being denied disability. He has grown up poor his whole life, has been disappointed many times, abandoned more than once, abused a couple of times, bullied, blamed for things that weren't his fault, and teased for his differences and quirks. Yet through all these trials and triumphs, he has remained standing—even after losing half of his pelvic bone and right hip joint, he still stands tall with the help of his cane.

Bobby's interests don't stop at web design; he's also a photographer, with his art available on RedBubble.com, and he loves creating videos on TikTok. His real dream is to go to school for cinematography, but for now, that will have to wait until he has the money and time to pursue it.

I am incredibly proud of him for not giving up on me, Lucas, or himself. I know that in time, people will see how truly talented and wonderful he is. He has so much to offer the world!

Therapy Today 3/2024

I've been seeing a therapist for a year now. It started with weekly sessions for several months, then every two weeks, and this year, it's been every two weeks to once a month. We've even discussed the possibility of discharge. Today, my therapist reminded me of where I began: when she first met me, my mom was actively attending my appointments, and I was extremely quiet, overly medicated, and still in a state of psychosis. I wouldn't answer any of her questions. She said my appearance was unkempt and that I didn't seem to be taking care of myself.

After six months of therapy, she noticed small signs of improvement, but I was still working with my psychiatrist to get my medication right. My therapist said she didn't see real progress until "Octoberish" of 2023. She observed that my attitude and moods had shifted after I started taking Quetiapine in August. She mentioned that I was opening up a lot more, answering questions, and engaging in conversation.

Beyond what my therapist has seen, I've noticed significant improvement since August 2023, thanks to my medication. It has helped balance me out and allowed my brain to produce the serotonin and dopamine I need to function in daily life. I'm bathing regularly now! I have a positive attitude, and I'm smiling and laughing again! I'm listening to music again, engaging in social activities, and setting both short-term and long-term goals. I have wants and dreams again.

Before, when I was depressed and in a low mania, I had given up on myself and everything. I had no hope. I felt isolated and lost. But praise be to God! Thanks to my doctors and medication, I am so much better now—that difficult time is behind me. I am now fully aware of my mood disorder, recognize the symptoms, and have resources to help when I need it. I am grateful for this progress and am looking forward to what's ahead!

It's Called Spiritual Growth, Baby Girl!

My good friend from Nigeria, Chris Vahe, has been sending me scripture passages, praying for me, and acting like the big brother I never had. He has been encouraging me to start tithing. To be honest, I've never actually tithed in my entire life. I've put small amounts into the offering plate here and there, but I've never truly tithed. I have given to charities and helped those in need when I was able to. Recently, Chris sent me Malachi 3:9-12, which essentially says that by not tithing, we are robbing the Lord, as our money isn't really ours— it's the Lord's. Some may disagree with this, and that's okay! Even if we can't give a full ten percent, the Lord knows our hearts and values whatever we can give, wherever we can.

Chris also shared 1 Corinthians 9:6-7: "Remember this: Whoever sows sparingly will also reap sparingly, and whoever sows generously will also reap generously. Each of you should give what you have decided in your heart to give, not reluctantly or under compulsion, for God loves a cheerful giver."

The Lord doesn't want anyone to give with reluctance, resentment, or out of obligation. He desires that we give out of love and compassion for others, with sincerity in our hearts.

TGIF

Today, I hustled hard with DoorDashing and did well. I also got a new job—another waitressing gig, but I'm dashing until my training starts. I was about to faint from not eating while delivering, so I decided to grab some sesame chicken at one of my stops. On the way home, I opened my fortune cookie, already feeling it would be a good one, and

I was right! It confirmed my beliefs and affirmations are on their way.

My fortune read: "You will exceed even your own expectations!" I just smiled, then went to pick up Lucas from school.

My Favorite Poem

I'm sharing my favorite poem, *The Road Not Taken* by Robert Frost, because I think a lot of people can relate to it. I've taken many roads less traveled myself, and it's truly been a journey! Would I change anything? No, because every experience has shaped me into the person I am today. I've been through so much and learned a lot along the way!

St. Patty's Day Eviction

Well, it's Redemption Year!! Bobby and I just got kicked out of my parents' house. In all honesty, I was behind on paying my mom rent for the past few months, but as soon as I began my new job, I was going to resume giving her money and catch up on what I owed her. I know who was really behind the influence of this whole operation. They made us sign a 30-day notice (about 4 and a half weeks), saying that we've been there long enough. Hello?!!! We know that!

I am not one for confrontation at all. My stepdad's very words were that, by us being there all these years, we "stole their retirement." How does one even "steal" someone's retirement? Sure, I know the power bill went up with us there, but it's not like we dipped into their savings or had access to my stepfather's 401(k) plan. Complete ludicrousness— it just did not make any sense to me whatsoever!

My mom came upstairs so I could sign after Bobby had signed. She tried talking to me, but I was angry. She tried to throw the word "mania" in my face, but I was just showing natural emotion. I told her to let me be so I wouldn't say anything ugly. We had already planned on leaving soon! They explained that they had worked extra hard over the years to save for retirement and that their retirement funds had diminished because we had been there, that we had drained them financially and caused stress in their marriage by staying in their home too long.

How's this for drama?

Looks like our new beginning on our own will be a bumpy one, but I'm sure we'll manage just fine!

Cards In The Mail

I have been receiving cards in the mail from Shelley at the mental health institute.

Here lately, she has sent me a Valentine's Day card and a St. Patty's Day card. She really is such a sweet person. I'll never forget her kindness towards me when I was her roommate while I was there. I've been meaning to send her a card in return because I know how miserable it can be being stuck in there with the same routine over and over, and how important it is for morale to look forward to the little things such as cards, chocolate bars, and sodas. Until you get certain freedoms taken away from you, you never realize how much you take for granted daily and how grateful you should be for what you have and for those around you that love you.

Being A Good Samaratin

Despite what I've been working on and going through, the Indian owner at the gas station asked me personally if I could give one of his employees/roommates a ride to and from work, so I obliged. I didn't mind at all. I told him I would help as much as I could until I started my new job. The guy was a hardworking person; he just didn't have transportation.

Remember how I mentioned my friend Kris Birmingham when I was in the hospital? How he brought me something to eat? Well, when I was in the mental health institute, his car had broken down, and my car was just sitting at home collecting dust, not being used, so I allowed him to borrow my car for three weeks. This way, he could save money on a rental until he could find a new vehicle. We had lost contact with one another after I had gotten out of the hospital, but when I returned to Facebook, we reconnected.

I'm really grateful for him because he's a true good Samaritan. He does little check-in text messages on me to make sure I'm doing alright, mainly because he knows where I've been mentally, and I'm sure he doesn't want to see me go through that again!

So, my note for the day is: be a good Samaritan! Help someone out where and when you can!

Bobby's Body Now

His scars are legendary—they truly are! They most definitely tell a story. They start from the mid part of his back, go all the way around down to his groin area, and across his abdomen. He also has a scar on his inner right thigh.

The past few years, Bobby has been cancer-free—praise the Lord! He has been able to walk with the help of his cane, and now he's getting back into the gymnasium! I'm so proud of him. He is working to regain upper body strength because he relies on those muscles a lot. He's even started using the bicycle slowly, pedaling to exercise his legs. There is some equipment he's still unable to use, but that's okay! I believe he's doing this not only to improve his physical strength but also to feel good about his body again and to boost his self-confidence and self-esteem.

Which is great! After all, it's **a proven fact that** exercise **is** beneficial **for** both **physical and mental health. Every doctor out there will tell you to** incorporate **some type of physical activity or exercise** into your routine.

3/21

Today was supposed to be a day of inspiration, but by the afternoon, it turned into a day of tears. Bobby made the decision to go live with his brother, asked me to find a friend to stay with, and suggested that Lucas stay with my mom and stepdad. Basically, he feels like separating is what's best.

I wrote to him:

"I want you. Ever since we met, I have always wanted you. Yes, we have been through a lot these past few years, been sort of separate because of sleeping arrangements, but I've always given you your space because you like a lot of space. I've been trying to be more intimate with you this year and have enjoyed kissing you more. I am—or still am—looking forward to you having your surgery. That is what is missing from our relationship: intimacy.

I just don't **understand why you believe separating is the best for the three of us. Do I need to get down on my hands and knees and beg you not to do this? Why** haven't **you forgiven me? What happened to 'together,** always'? **What happened to our tattoos from our honeymoon?"**

When I got home, we spoke. I did get down on my knees in front of him. He showed no emotion. He couldn't show any emotion— all he had was anger, bitterness, logic, and reason. And fear.

Fear that I'm going to turn back into a manic person. Fear that I'm going to continue to hurt him.

He kept telling me that he felt the best thing was to separate. He said he needed to set out and finish school, to make something of himself without anything or anyone holding him back anymore. He said he needs his soul to heal. He needs time to breathe.

Middle Of The Night Entry

I woke up at 2 a.m. and couldn't go back to sleep, so of course, I spoke to my friends in Nigeria about what was going on. They felt my pain and were crying with me, even from miles away. I just laid here, praying to God to give me strength to get through all of this—whatever "this" is. Chris Vahe told me to rebuke any evil, so I did.

Timo is sick with typhoid, but he was still being a good friend, listening with an open ear and doing his best to encourage me. I wish I could help Timo. I wish I had the money to send him for medicine or food. I wish I could take him some soup to help him feel better. My heart is aching.

It's almost 6 a.m. now. Earlier, I listened to *For King and Country's* **song,** *"Shoulders."* I listen to that song whenever I feel down and need a pick-me-up. I also listened to Lauren Daigle's song, *"You Say."* She has such a beautiful voice. Her song is so powerful because it reminds us of what God thinks of us and how much He loves us.

I realized I forgot to take my medicine last night, which was not a good thing. One night isn't going to hurt me, but I most definitely can't let it become a habit. I sent Lauren's song to Lindsay the other day as a reminder for her—because we all need reminders of God's love for us.

God's love for us is unwavering and immense! We cannot fathom the unconditional love that the Lord has for each of us!

As of right now, I am trying to collect myself because a new day is about to begin, and I've got to remain strong. Earlier, I thought about the tattoo on the top of my right foot. It's **a sunflower with** Psalms 31:24:

"Be strong and courageous, all you who hope in the Lord."

Friday Continued

I sobbed off and on all day. Talked to a good friend that is a strong God-fearing woman. I attempted to DoorDash today but didn't have any luck; I basically made my money back that I spent on gasoline. I messaged Bobby today and got no response from him whatsoever. I texted my mom to let her know what was going on so that she was aware of everything.

Later that afternoon, she came home, and we talked upstairs. She told me that she would help me out and that she wasn't abandoning me, but I needed to help myself out and stand on my own two feet. That the reason why they evicted us is because we simply have been in their home too long!

My heart goes out to the royal family, and my prayers for Kate Middleton and the family have been lifted up. I will continue to think of them and pray for them as they are going through this difficult time. CANCER SUCKS! I know. So many others can RELATE to this and understand this just as much as I continue to tell my story.

The night ended with my mom hugging me, which was nice.

Saturday March 23

I've been resting today. Mentally drained, so I slept the first half of the day. Speaking from experience, make sure you take care of your mental health so that you can function properly and don't spiral into depression! Make sure you reach out to others and talk about your situation and don't isolate yourself! You're not alone!

So far, I'm not having any luck finding someone to let me stay with them so I can save up money for a room for rent. I really hate this. All this uncertainty. This isn't how I pictured our redemption year.

However, I'm not crying today. I begin my new job on Monday at a corporate Italian restaurant, which I'm excited about. I have a lot of restaurant experience; that is most of what my work experience has been in—the restaurant industry. Hospitality is my middle name!

I took Food & Hospitality in high school. I have always had a passion for serving others, mainly because of my Christian upbringing and my love for the Lord and others. I take pleasure in serving others with food and seeing them happy eating. I enjoy dining out with my family and friends, so when I serve, I like to give good service to customers and give them a good experience as well and make them happy.

It's all a part of fellowship too! Fellowship with other Christians is so important because not only do we get to break bread together, but we get to share our lives with one another—our concerns, our needs. Praying together is important!

Hope on Palm Sunday

Well, on Palm Sunday, I'll be honest, I skipped church. I do not go every Sunday like I probably should. I ended up hustling and DoorDashing. I drove around the city of Suffolk from 8 a.m. until about 2 p.m. In the end, I made out decent. To make any money in a dash, you literally have to do it for hours and make several deliveries to bring in decent money. When I got home, I spoke to my friends in Nigeria for a bit, and I was beginning to get concerned that I wasn't going to find anyone to let me stay with them temporarily so I could save up some money until I could find a place. Then, the least likely person I could think of came to mind. It's someone I went to high school with, and they had asked me a long time ago to watch their newborn baby twins so they could have a fun night out, and I had obliged. It's funny because, during that time, I was also going through a tough time. Well, I told this person about my situation, and he just said, "When can we expect you? Our doors are always open to those in need." This individual isn't even a Christian, but he has such a good heart and is genuinely a good person. I just said, "God bless you!" I was so relieved and incredibly grateful that I had a friend willing to take me in while I saved up enough money to find a room to rent, a place of my own, or at least figure something out.

Prior to this breakthrough, I met up with Bobby in the Dollar Tree parking lot, where he was quietly doing his homework. I needed to speak to him and confront him about where we stood. I needed to know if there was hope for us. Bobby basically said that he felt like it was best that we spend some time apart, that he would still talk to me and still help me financially, but we'd have to wait and see how things pan out. He told me that maybe it was a good thing for me to learn to stand on my own two feet for a change because we both grew up very differently. Here's a little bit of backstory about how we grew up: Bobby grew up rough/poor in Portsmouth with a single mom and three brothers. On the contrary, I grew up very privileged—I had everything handed to me. My mother held my hand way too much. Honestly, I was spoiled. I wasn't taught how to be independent. Anyway, Bobby hugged me, and at the end of the day, I felt much better because I had hope in my heart. I had a place to go, and I had hope for our marriage. I pray that the Lord can help restore our marriage because marriage isn't easy—it takes hard work.

Monday

I've requested a lot of prayers from several people that are prayer warriors to pray for our marriage. I started orientation for my new job today, and I received a lot of pamphlets. I feel like I'm back in school for hospitality—whew! All of this for a restaurant! But I am going to learn everything and make it fun.

I went to a counseling appointment today, and my mom came along. It felt a little awkward having her there with me. She listened to how I was feeling. My counselor told me I needed to have a goal or game plan for how long I was going to stay with my friend so I don't overstay my welcome. I voiced something that had been bothering me about my mom during the session: she isn't supporting me in the way I wish she would. But it's because we both have different personalities and think very differently.

Well, I've decided to still show kindness, care, and love toward my husband, despite everything that is going on and his decision to go stay with his brother and split up our family. I'm going to continue to pray for him, do my best at my new job, and fix the things that I need to fix. I'm only human. We're all human and make mistakes.

I have a mood disorder, and I struggle with attention issues, reasoning, listening, getting irritated, and not speaking, among other things. All I can say is that I know I'm not alone, and I am sure there are many others out there who have the same issues that I have.

Praising the Lord this Wednesday

Today was a good day. Today is the day that the Lord has made, let us rejoice and be glad in it! I got up and spoke to Timo and Chris, my Nigerian buddies, which was a nice way to start the day. I went to my usual coffee spot and gave the Indian guy a ride home. After that, I took Lucas to school and began my scheduled dash for the day. It turned out to be a pretty decent dash overall.

Midday, Bobby called me and said he wasn't having much luck. He also mentioned that he needed some money for gas, so I told him I'd meet him and give him my card so he could put enough in his tank to continue his dash. When we met, Bobby touched my hand and asked if I was cold, since the weather was a bit chilly, but I said no. Before I left to go on my next order, I leaned into his car window, and he let me give him a peck on the lips.

This evening, I just cooked breakfast for dinner—nothing special, but comforting nonetheless. Bobby had gone to the gym, but when he returned, he came in to talk to me and gave me a hug, which was really nice. It makes me feel so much better knowing that there is hope for our marriage. We've just been through so much hell. We've been through so much pain.

**Poem For Bobby, Honoring Christina Perry's 1000 Years &
Also Our Wedding Song**

I have loved you for a thousand years.
Remember when I asked you, "Is that everything you want?"
I will love you for a thousand more.
Your thoughts in your mind were "No."

Hell brought us together, hell tore us apart;
Wounds bring on more tears.
Redemption's year is like shutting a door.

I will be brave, facing what stands in front of me.
My heart beats fast with colors and promises—
Of everything that's in store.
Babe, don't be afraid.

I have died every day waiting for you.
I will be with you through every high and low.
I have loved you for a thousand years,
And I will love you for a thousand more.

"Together, Always."

Easter Sunday 2024

Well, I woke up and gave the Indian guy a ride home. I attempted to tell him the meaning of Easter and share with him about Jesus, but he didn't really seem to care. Still, praise be to God! Our Lord Jesus Christ is risen!

I can't help but think about the Easter I experienced two years ago with my anointing. This Easter was very different. To be honest, I am exhausted and not in a very good mood. That said, I am grateful to have the day off and to have spent time with loved ones.

My family came over, and it was a very simple holiday. We all got together and ate hamburgers, hot dogs, potato salad, deviled eggs, and pies from the church. Bobby chose to work today, and his absence left me feeling a bit sad. I did my best not to be angry with him and instead tried to understand and be supportive. I saved him a plate and hugged him when he returned home.

Easter ended with a beautiful sunset, peaceful goodnights, and a much-needed restful night's sleep.

April Fool's Day

I've never been a prank player or a joker. I do my best to be funny, but I'm more of a serious person than anything. Chris Vahe, who is from Nigeria, and I spoke this morning, as we usually do. We have dreams and visions of hopefully beginning organizations to help others in need one day. We are both like-minded and believe that God has huge things in store for the both of us. We are very different in a lot of regards, but in some ways, we share many of the same values. We have already learned a lot from each other, even though we are oceans apart and millions of miles away. He has become like a brother to me — the kind I've never had.

Friday April 5th

Donate Day!

I donated some clothes to Goodwill, and I gave my jewelry armoire to an old friend who used to work with my mom. When I visited this woman, she recalled the time that I spoke with her back when I was manic and felt opressed. She looked at me and told me she had been trying to get through to me, but I was simply not there. She said she had been praying for me. Thank God for her prayers.

Thank you, Lord, for the people who prayed for me! All I can say is, thank God for my life and that I am alive — that I did not take my life, because I am anointed! I have a divine purpose in this life and in this world!

I am strong through Jesus Christ! I have strong, amazing, and admirable ancestors! I am a child of God! I am Samantha Bond!

I am finishing the day by studying all the ingredients on the menu at the new restaurant so I can do my job properly and be prepared to tell our guests what each dish has in it. I'm very excited to provide exceptional service, hospitality as well as make great money ahead!

Spiritual Warfare

Most seasoned Christians are familiar with the topic of spiritual warfare, but many in the younger generation are not. A lot of them still don't fully understand the importance of prayer, praying fervently, or battling in the spirit. The main reason for spiritual warfare is to pray and battle for God's kingdom against Satan's kingdom. Now that I am well, or at least much better again, I am making sure that I am reading scripture, attending church regularly, and praying.

Superb Sunday 4/7

Bobby had gone camping with his brothers up in Prince William Park for the weekend. Before his departure, I told him to be safe (of course) and to have a good time, because he deserved a weekend away. All Sunday morning, I got up, went to 7-11, and got my normal cup of joe. I even gave the Indian guy there a ride home. Then, I came back and just laid in bed to rest. I ended up skipping service—my body needed rest, and my mind needed rest too.

I fiddled around online, like a lot of folks do. I also sent my husband some sweet, romantic reminisce videos from the past. I told him I missed him. I studied for my menu test for work. That afternoon, Bobby came home looking exhausted, but I gave him a big hug. Lucas had already greeted him downstairs.

I continued to speak with Bobby in our room and closed the door behind me. He had just gotten out of the shower, and I'll admit I was trying to initiate putting the moves on my husband. We shared intimacy in a way that only strengthened our bond, kissing passionately. After it was over, I began to sob emotionally in his arms. At first, he didn't understand why I was crying.

I told him I was so sorry for not being there before, back when I was oppressed, and that I missed him. I truly missed my husband's affection—his gentle touch, his embrace, his kisses—I missed all of it. I hadn't realized just how much until that moment. Bobby asked, "You missed me that much?" I sobbed, "Yes."

That evening, on the way to work to take my menu test, I just thanked the Lord and thought to myself: *Wow, the healing process has begun. We need to heal, and I need to heal too.'*

Matthew 19:6 says, "So they are no longer two, but one flesh. Therefore, what God has joined together, let no one separate."

With any relationship, it takes work. Marriage takes work. It's the same with our relationship with God! You cannot expect to call on God only when you need Him! God doesn't work like that! The Lord wants you to be with Him daily. He wants you to thank Him, praise Him, talk to Him like He's your best friend, give Him your worries, read His word, follow His commandments, be kind, pray, and be of service to others.

Fan Friday 4/12

The past couple of days, I have been resting. Mentally, I've been exhausted. Yesterday, my copy of Trent Shelton's new book, *Protect Your Peace,* came in the mail. I had already begun to read it. On the way to pick Lucas up from school, something unexpected happened — I hopped on one of Trent's live streams on FB at just the right moment.

It truly was music to my ears. He spoke about how we should all take a moment to be proud of ourselves and how far we've come. He spoke through the video as if he was speaking to each individual personally, saying, "I'm proud of you!"

The truth is, I have come a long way. This year—our redemption year—is not looking how I pictured it at all. But I have made significant progress with my mental health. I've even kept the demons away! I don't want any more demons in my doorway. I am proud of myself. I love myself again. I am doing things I enjoy again. I am proud of Bobby too.

I want to live to the fullest! I want to learn more and grow. I am keeping my head held high and marching forward. Just like Trent says in his book, "I Declare War!" Today has been a blessing. Trent, you are a blessing. Thank you, brother.

Shipping Out Saturday

Today, we packed up our belongings and moved them into a storage unit—basically a bedroom's worth of stuff: dresser, bed, tables, bookcase, books, movies, and other miscellaneous items. Moving is a pain in the neck, but thankfully the pastor of the church and Bobby's two brothers helped.

In a sense, leaving this home is like a death to me. This has been my home since I was seventeen years old, off and on. Almost half of my adult life has been spent in this house.

Not only were we being kicked out of the place that has been so familiar to me all these years, but I also found out that my stepdad made the decision to change the locks. We've been coming and going all these years, and suddenly, the locks are being changed? Now, if I want to come by, I have to call or knock on the door. The doors aren't wide open any longer.

The place where I created memories and found refuge—comfort—was suddenly ripped away.

Backtracking

Today was going to be our first day being separated, the three of us. Before picking Lucas up from school, Mom brought up the subject of taking temporary guardianship of him since he was going to be living with them. I told her it was unnecessary. I explained that I was only 15 minutes away and Bobby was 30 minutes away in case of an emergency.

I even gave her his health insurance cards to make copies. But still, she kept on with her "what if" scenarios. It got me upset. I told her nothing was going to happen to us.

She said, "You don't know that!" So, I raised my voice and called her a 'Negative Nancy'—not once, but twice!

My mentality was simple: I am walking by faith. I am not going to walk around every day thinking I'm going to die, get hit by a bus, or have something terrible happen. Bobby and I have already been through enough hell. I want to take each day as it comes.

Truth Tuesday

Bloody hell, life doesn't always go the way you plan. You may plan something, and it gets altered. One vice that's been getting me through this year, besides my medication, is vaping. Yeah, I started vaping again. It helps me relax, and I enjoy all the flavors. Yes, I know it's not good for you—anyways, don't judge.

Another truth bomb for the day is that I got so angry with Bobby today because he canceled his Duke appointment that I was supposed to go to with him. These appointments are scheduled six months out in advance—you just don't cancel this type of scan checkup. I yelled at Bobby out in the driveway for canceling and asked him WHY? I told him, "I told you not to!" His fear of my parents throwing the rest of our belongings out at the end of the road was the reason.

I proceeded to go to work, and on my way, I just broke down and cried. I cried out, "Yeshua," four times and just spoke about how I was feeling. Then, I wiped my tears and went to work. Later that afternoon, I picked up Lucas from school, and when Bobby got home from work, he was finishing up cleaning and packing. I apologized to him for yelling and for getting so angry.

Sunday, April 21

As a fan and supporter of Trent, I receive community text messages randomly here and there. This morning, I got one saying how proud Trent is of me and about the future I am about to create! It made me smile and also made me think about For King and Country's song, *Unity*. Love connects us all. Unity is what we need.

This Sunday, I made the decision to visit a different house of God. A friend from another church we both used to attend had been going there and had nothing but great things to say about it, so I went. I'm glad I did. I swear, no lie, it felt as if God had led me there on this exact day to hear this message because it was like it was meant specifically for me! I'm sure others benefited from the message as well, but man, it was spot on!

The message was about the pressures of life. The pastor used 1 Corinthians 9:24, Philippians 3:14, Acts 26-28, and Jeremiah 1:12 & 29:11. As for me, I was certainly feeling pressure from every angle a person could feel pressured in. I felt like I was in a Ninja pressure cooker even, lol. He gave everyone seven takeaways for the week, and I have to share because sharing is caring:

1. Keep your eyes and ears on God

2. Encourage others with what God says

3. Live your life with thanksgiving

4. Help build a fire

5. Shake off the demonic attacks

6. Shake off the opinions of others

7. Shake off the need to explain yourself

I left feeling better and renewed. The rest of the day, I took it easy. I had been working hard and mentally needed a break, so I brought Lucas back to my friend's place where I was staying and let him play with her twin boys. I curled up on the sofa and read my copy of *Protect Your Peace*. Later, it was time to take Lucas back to my mom's. At least I knew where he was going and that he was safe there.

I wish I could be with him at night so I could read to him. I know I'm not the perfect parent, but I do make it a point to read to my son. For the rest of the evening, as any normal American would do, I chilled watching Netflix, ate a burger and fries, and watched one of my all-time favorites: *You've Got Mail* with Tom Hanks & Meg Ryan. They were wonderful in that film! "Don't you just love New York in the fall? I would send you a bouquet of newly sharpened pencils!"

Late Night Popcorn

I decided to open the welcome package from the church I had visited, and it included popcorn. A little note was attached! Remember how I just said that I felt like God led me to this church on purpose? Well, the note said, "It's true, because we believe that your steps are ordered by God! You are not here by accident—you are here by Divine Appointment!" It continues further on than that, but I kept it short and sweet, to the point.

Tears at Bdubs

We decided to meet at Buffalo Wild Wings to see each other. Our so-called date turned into a painful discussion in a dark corner. My wings didn't taste the greatest anymore.

Bobby proceeded to ask me what the next step was, and I just looked at him with my usual sad puppy dog eyes. I replied, "What do you mean? We're going to try and find a place together in a month or so, so we can all be together…"

He gloated, "What if I don't want that?" He continued to tell me how he felt. He brought up the past, his fears of the future, and a lot of other things. I just sat there in tears. I told him, "You can't do this to me. You are my heart and soul."

It was as if I was using an emotional heart defibrillator from across the table, but I was getting a flatline. No pulse. "We've invested almost eight years together; I don't want to see us flush it down the drain," I said. Tonight was painful. I just prayed to God and gave the situation to Him while driving back to where I was currently staying.

Calling on Friends

I tried to ring my boo Brooke first, but she couldn't talk because her babies were sick. I needed a lifeline quickly, so I called her. When she wasn't available, I didn't know who else to turn to except my good friend Chris Vahe in Nigeria. Thank God he was still awake.

He answered, and I just said his name once before I started to sob. He could feel my pain through the phone from thousands of miles away. I told him how Bobby was treating me and how Bobby did not have Christ in his heart. We kept talking, and Chris said we must take matters to his pastor, Prophet, right away. By the grace of God, I got back to my friend's house safely, especially after being so emotional.

Satan loves to attack our minds.

It was my second time visiting this new church, and I really loved it! I truly believed the message today. It just so fits my whole story and even current events right now. The message was about "Why is the mind a battlefield?" First, because it's part of our decision-making. Secondly, it's one of Satan's best tactics, and Thirdly, it's a way for worldly influences to infiltrate our minds.

The pastor went on about how an evil notion/thought can transform into evil actions or sinful behavior. First, there's the presentation of that thought/notion. Next is a consideration; the third is conception, which means turning those thoughts into an emotional engagement, for example, hate, anger, lust, etc. Then, there comes Intention, where you begin planning it out or start acting upon it, which turns into Execution, which means you have fully committed the act.

Whether it is a crime, cheating on your spouse, stealing something, blackmailing someone, or whatever it may be, this is when you should be prepared to face the consequences. It's not physical consequences all the time, either. It can mean spiritual consequences as well. Last is Habituation. Where the evil notions/acts/ sinful behaviors become habitual, and you keep repeating them over and over.

I am not here to judge anyone or condemn anyone. I am here to tell you about my personal experiences with being oppressed and in such a low mania that the devil and his demonic forces had a foothold over my mind. I am here to tell you that it is very real, and if you do not believe in it is your choice. We must keep our minds protected and strong from the enemy because that is where he attacks us the most!

Just another manic Monday

Most people dread the new week; Monday again? The weekend always seems to fly by, with never enough time to catch a break. Virginia was in full swing of springtime, the yellow pollen thickening everywhere. Well, I felt like dog poo. My allergies were kicking me in the butt! Everyone I spoke to, everywhere I went, had their allergies bothering them as well. I am a social butterfly, as you can tell. Always have been.

However, I grunted and stretched, got up anyway, and continued onto my morning routine to 7-11 to fetch my cup of coffee and give my

Indian friend a ride home. Then, I pursued to ride over to my mother's home, which was no longer my home. It still feels very weird having to call her or text her to let me in, but I was still coming over and waking up Lucas, getting him ready for school, and taking him to school. After that, I had a Dash scheduled for the day, so I hustled while sneezing as I drove all over Suffolk feeling crappy making deliveries.

Later that afternoon, when it was time to head back to my friend's place, my favorite group, For King & Country's song Unsung Hero, came on the radio. I just smiled, and this guy on his motorcycle in front of me was doing this funky dance which was making me chuckle. He seemed to be enjoying his ride. I protected my peace for the rest of the evening by curling up with some comfort food and watching one of my favorite movies, the Holiday. I could never get tired of that film.

Therapy & Thankful Tuesday 4/30

I have always viewed myself as the Disney character of Mulan. The reason is that Mulan was expected to be something she was not. She was much more than that; her destiny was different. Also, her father told her that she was like one of the flowers on the cherry blossom trees; it was late, but when it blooms, it will be the most beautiful of all. I have always considered myself a late-blooming flower, and I have never been a follower for good reason. I wasn't born to be a follower. I was born to be a leader. The Lord will guide me on how to lead and what I need to do. My hope and trust are in the Lord. Bobby and I have both been through a lot in our lives and these past few years, as you can tell. We are both survivors, warriors even. Therapy went well today; I still go because therapy never hurts anyone. Even the most successful people in the world go to therapy or have been in therapy at some point in their lives.

Please do not ever be ashamed of ever needing to reach out to someone for help or therapy. It is a place of refuge. Therapy is a safe place for you to vent, grow, learn, and even process your emotions in a healthy manner.

Some people have their mottos and own personal mantras that they live by. Well, I have come up with my own this year. I call it my three P's.

MY 3 P's

Prayer

- Keeping you connected to God; all about relationships.

- Thanksgiving/praise.

- Giving our worries and concerns to God.

- Prayer is our best weapon against the enemy, Satan.

Positivity

- Reading the living word of God and all of God's promises for our life.

- Our thoughts and attitudes control everything.

Perseverance

- What does the bible say about perseverance? James 1:12 says, "Blessed is the one who perseveres under trial because having stood the test, that person will receive the crown of life that the Lord has promised to those who love him."

- Galatians 6:9 says, "And let us not grow weary of doing good, for in due season we will reap if we do not give up."

- The point is not to give up because even though we may be going through a tough season, some of our best days are ahead. Each season of our life is different. The devil doesn't want you to persevere. He wants you to give up and throw in the towel. Jeremiah 29:11 says, "For I know the plans I have for you," declares the Lord, "plans to prosper you not to harm you, plans to give you hope and a future."

Tuesday 5/14

It was another day of hustling and working before I went to work, Dashing. The week before had been a rough week of working diligently and, mixed emotions, and yes, even a mental breakdown. Yes, even though I am better and stronger again with everything going on, I had a bad day and just broke down. Anyways, while I was dashing, the holy spirit just spoke to me, and I wheeled into a gas station and parked immediately. I began to call out to God and started crying. I brought out my spiritual heart defibrillators, closed my eyes, pumped them mid-air onto Bobby's spiritual heart 4 times, and cried out to God to save Bobby, bring my husband back!

Bring him back to me, Lord! Heal him, God! The man in the SUV next to me glanced over and saw me as I prayed. I proceeded to roll down my window. He asked if I was okay. I told him that I was battling for my husband. He just said, "Trust God that everything is going to be okay. He has everything under control." So, I wiped my tears and carried on. Later, God instructed me to write Bobby a letter telling him how I felt and to go ahead and give him the poem I wrote. Even though it was meant to be a surprise, it was important to give it to him now.

5/19/2024

It was a morning of pure hell. I woke up super early, and oddly, my scalp was itching. I proceeded to go to the bathroom to take a shower because I planned on going to service. Well, when I had gone into the bathroom and undressed, I noticed that my belly was covered in raised red splotches. I had broken out in hives. I left my friend's house and gave my Indian friend a ride home like I had been doing for the past couple of months. He was worried, but I was trying to shrug it off as if I was going to be fine.

I went out to my brother-in-law's home, where Bobby was then residing, and I was going to take Lucas, but I began to feel worse. I started getting a migraine, and the hives were all over my body. My brother-in-law commented that Jesus would forgive me for missing service by going to get seen. True. Well, I left, headed back to Suffolk, and went straight to the emergency room.

When I got there, I was feeling very sick. They took me back right away, and I vomited while the guy was trying to do bloodwork on me. And, of course, me, being an older woman and after having a child, you just can't control your bowels any longer; you sneeze, cough, or in my case vomited, I pissed myself. It was embarrassing. But, hey, Nurses are used to seeing all sorts of things like this, right? I had already called them out of work earlier that morning and told them that I was going to the E.R. There was no way I could work in my condition. After the E.R., I went back to my friend's house and slept.

Bobby's Surgery 5/20

The next day, I did not feel any better. I still felt very ill. I was covered head to toe and itching like crazy!! But that day, my husband needed me. He was having a very important surgery. He was having his penile pump implant surgery. We had gotten to the hospital early, as requested. Knowing how doctors are, they are never on time for anything, so we waited until it was time.

They finally called him back to the room for prep. It was getting closer to 2 pm. I had been dozing off and on in the waiting area with the blanket the nurses provided. I was not feeling well at all. I had not eaten since Saturday, and I could barely keep down water. I was feeling nauseated. Bobby's surgery took a couple of hours.

Finally, his doctor, a very pleasant fellow, came out and told me that his surgery was very successful. He told me that he was very pleased with the outcome! He told me that they tested the device while they were in there and that they were pleased with its overall functionality. That Bobby should be very pleased. We left the hospital with his pain medications, and I took my husband back to his brother's house so he could rest. Then, I headed back to Suffolk so I could rest as well.

Torture Tuesday

The next day, I got up, gave my Indian friend a ride home like I had been doing, and took Lucas to school. My body was still covered in hives. My face looked like bees had stung it. I decided to get Bobby something to drink and eat from Wawa and go check on him to make sure he was okay from his surgery the prior day. I drove all the way out to Chesapeake to see him.

We were out in the backyard sitting, and I brought up the subject of our living arrangements. Bobby basically told me that there was no "we" and that he wanted to get his own place and carry on his own. So I paused for a moment and then, point blank, asked him, "So, are we in this together or not?" He replied, "NO". He even told me that he did not sign up to marry or take care of a child, referencing me.

My heart sank. I kept my composure in front of him. I did not stay much longer after that. I left and went to my aunt and uncle's home to see my cousin DJ. He told me he wanted to give me some money that he felt like he owed me. Plus, I needed the money anyway. I stayed broke. I was living day by day and running on faith right now, relying on good 'Ol Jehovah Jireh.'

Anyway, when I got to my aunt and uncle's house, my cousin DJ was there with me and his arms wide open. Pain rushed in like I had never felt before, and my emotions let out. I sobbed hard. My heart hurt immensely. I went next door to my grandfather's to see him. He had broken his tailbone, poor man; he was 94 years old. He was the most intelligent person I knew, but his body was beginning to take its toll. I stayed for a bit. I had sat on the couch that belonged to my grandmother a long time ago; it was her space. It was her space where she usually crocheted.

To this very day, I still use the blanket that she crocheted me to sleep with. It is special to me and can never be replaced. Before I left to return to Suffolk, I cried out to Yeshua! I asked Yeshua to hold my heart in his hands!

The Middle Of The Week

I do not like to lie to Lucas at all. I went ahead and told Lucas that his Daddy did not love Mommy anymore and that he wanted to leave me. Lucas's little heart was broken. He cried so hard and didn't understand why. That Friday, I had to work, so I had to take Lucas out to his dad so he could watch him. Lucas questioned his father why he didn't love me anymore. Bobby just said, "Well, that's a big kid kind of a question." I told him that I would be getting him back on Sunday, and Bobby commented that we were ruining his life. By him taking his son for the weekend? Ruining his life? I ignored him and kept my mouth shut.

That week, I had already been filled with anger, and maybe it was my bipolar disorder, or who knows maybe some women feel like this, but I really wanted to hit my husband in the face! For some of the things he had said to me and done to me, I wanted to hit him! Did I? No. Was I wrong for feeling these things? Yes and No. It was a natural human feeling. It was wrong for me to have anger or hate in my heart.

Sunday 5/26

This morning, I was finally able to go to service. I was in my car driving and speaking to God. God just clearly told me, "Samantha, quit fighting! I am fighting for you! Trust in me". So, I continued to pick up Lucas for service, and Bobby proceeded to give me a hug and a kiss. I embraced him and told him that I loved him even if he did not love me back. That is what unconditional love is. God loves us all even when we do not love God or show God that we love him in return. I invited him to service, but he told me that he was still sore and healing so that he would go soon.

Wednesday 5/29

Can I catch a Break? I woke up in excruciating pain. I could not move my right arm to save my life. I still got up and gave my Indian friend a ride home like I had been doing. I still went to my mom's house, got Lucas up and ready for school, and took him. Then, I went straight to urgent care. They gave me a shot in the hip and Toradol for the pain and inflammation. They said I could have pulled a muscle or pinched a nerve.

They took me to the other room to x-ray my shoulder. The next day, which was Thursday, the doctor's office called me and told me that radiology had taken a closer look at my x-ray and said it looked like I had partially dislocated my shoulder. All this from sleeping on it wrong? Sleeping on a stiff sofa, SMDH.

Saturday, June 1ˢᵗ

New Month. New Me. New Beginnings. I decided to take matters into my own hands. My boss did not give me any hours after I told her weeks ago of my circumstances. So I did not show up for my shift. I scheduled a door dash shift for Saturday night instead.

Boy, I'm glad I did. I made $150 plus a $20 tip from a girl who worked at Amazon. I choose to dash by the time. All I can say is Thank God for the company Door Dash and CEO & Cofounder Tony Xu. Companies like this give people like me the opportunity to work for themselves and create their own schedules.

Plus, I also became a brand partner for my favorite wellness company again, Fit Team Global. Christopher Hummel is the CEO and is a remarkable man who treats everyone in the company with recognition and compassion. We sell the best organic wellness products that are great for weight loss and just overall good for general health. Thirdly, as soon as I have the start-up money, which is soon, I will start my own travel agent business. I am great with people already and want to help people book their vacations and business trips while I get discounts on travel for being part of the company.

Why am I doing all of this? I have been wanting to go in the direction of working for ME, MYSELF, & SAMIAM for a while now! I do not want to have to answer anyone but myself. I am just going to say this OUT LOUD! Employers say they understand mental health needs, but they really don't. They do not understand the need to take time off work to go to countless psychiatrist or counseling appointments or to take mental health days or breaks. So, this is why I want to work for myself. I am holding myself accountable. I am my own motivator. I know what I need to do to get things done. I can be my own boss. I've got this!

Tyranny Tuesday

The day started off busy getting Lucas off to school. Then, I had an appointment with my psychiatrist. I noticed my phone was acting up with the internet and thought it was just a bad connection. Well, I noticed my messages to Chris Vahe were not going through at all.

I went back to my friend's house, and he had Wi-Fi, so all my messages came through. Then I tried to make calls, and that's when I found out that our phone service had been disconnected temporarily. I was freaking out a bit. I needed my phone. I couldn't call anyone or even door dash without my phone!

Well, it was the afternoon, and we had planned on meeting Bobby for dinner, so I picked up Lucas. Since I couldn't get in touch with him, we made the drive out to Chesapeake to reach him. We got there, and he was nowhere in sight. My brother-in-law and his wife were home, and they called Bobby's other brother to see if he was at his house, and of course, he was in Portsmouth. She told me that Bobby paid the bill, and our phones are back on, to turn the phone off and back on, and it should be active.

I immediately called Bobby and suggested that we come to Portsmouth to meet him for dinner, but he replied with a 'No' that it had been a bad day. Then he came at me, talking about separating our phone and car insurance bills and still speaking about separating from me. I go out to the front porch, and I get angry. I automatically jump at his throat with the fact that I have been nothing but kind to him all year long, loving and supportive, showing him that I love him so much. I have been doing so much better in a whole year. I called him out and told him that he hadn't been trying, that it was like he was giving up on me and us. He responded with fear and bitterness and told me that he didn't want to be under the control of the tyranny of my bipolar disorder!!???OH? The Tyranny of my bipolar disorder? I was livid.

I was upset because he wasn't being fair. He was using my disorder against me. I yelled at him and said, "You aren't the man I thought you were!" and hung up the phone! He tried calling me back. Of course, I didn't respond. I went out back crying because Bobby was being a huge donkey's ass! No, that's not a curse because "ass" is technically a donkey, lol.

Anyway, my brother-in-law's wife suggested I calm down before I drove off. Ten minutes later, I sent Bobby a text message and sent him Malachi 2:16, "The man who hates and divorces his wife," says the Lord, the God of Israel, "does violence to the one he should protect," says the Lord Almighty. So be on your guard, and do not be unfaithful". I told him, you can call me a Zealot and a bible thumper all you want, but I stand with Jesus. I am Yeshua's bride. I answer to God. God does not like divorce; Satan does, though!

A couple of days later

A friend of mine had done a practice run of makeup on my face. She did the whole work: brows, lashes, eye shadow, everything. Bobby had gotten Lucas from school and taken him back to his brother's place, but I was out dashing. I told him that I'd pick him up later. The only complaint about making deliveries is that after you accept an order, you cannot see where you are delivering to. Well, my last delivery for the evening was out to Norfolk. Another toll bill. Doordash doesn't help pay for toll bills. So, I called Bobby to let him know that I was going to be late getting a little. Well, it was about 9:15 until I got there. Bobby noticed my appearance and told me that I looked nice. I smiled on the inside. He allowed me to give him a hug before we left. He was being kind to me; that was a step in the right direction.

Tough Cookie

Today, I decided to get up with an old friend who does ink out of her house. She's been doing tattoo work for thirteen years. It was late in the afternoon; Lucas and I made the trip out into the country where she resided. I decided to get the words, Tough Cookie inked onto my arm in honor of my grandmother Reed because that's what some people referred to her as because of something she had to endure. As a reminder, my grandmother was left with four children to raise by herself because my grandfather committed suicide. Anyway, I believe that since I am her granddaughter and because of the challenges and things that I have faced in my life, I have deserved the name Tough Cookie as well. Those are stories for different times, I promise.

7 June, My birthday

Tripping on my birthday. No lie. First thing in the a.m. I tripped out of the door on the dog rope! Man! I fell, and thank God I didn't break anything. I got up, brushed myself off, and just kept going and didn't let it ruin my day. I worked on my birthday. I dashed proudly and made my deliveries, vaped away, listened to K-Love radio station, and just rode around Harborview. The afternoon came quickly, and I picked up Lucas from school. I dropped him off with my mom. She had agreed to watch him for the night so I could go out for my birthday.

I was going out to celebrate my birthday! After all, I had been sick for the past few years and hadn't truly celebrated. My high school buddy, Deidre "Dee," had re-connected over a couple of years, and she and her boyfriend were treating me out for the night. We went to this local bar in town. Well, we had a decent time, but boy, did we feel out of place! It was Biker's night, lol. There were like 50+ bikers there giving the Bro hugs, shaking hands, drinking beers, and smoking their cigs outside....

Well, I turned Dee onto blue motorcycles, lol. Even though I wasn't supposed to drink alcohol, I chose to have one night of cutting loose for a change. I am an adult. I know what I can handle. I know what addiction is. I know not to make a habit out of it. Well, we played some pool, and Dee wanted some greasy bar food, but their fryer broke down, so we left and went to another local bar in town.

We ate nachos. I had steamed shrimp and cheered with our tall, angry orchards, and then she helped me with my birthday cookie skillet.

6/9/2024

Bobby was supposed to go to church with Lucas and me, but he backed out and said he had homework to do. He had dropped the web design thing and decided to go to school for what he truly wanted all along. He was attending Full Sail University for Cinematography. I was happy he chose to do that, but I was not very pleased he was not making time for the Lord. I did my best not to get angry. Lucas stayed with him, and I went to service alone. The Service was great! This sermon is too good not to share! Pastor talked about his wisdom nuggets and how the word of God is our anchor!

1) Face your Fears!! Isiah 41:10 & 2 Timothy 1:7

2) Forget your Failures!! Philippians 3 12-14

3) Focus your Faith!! Hebrews 12 1-2

Then the pastor used a quote by Max Lucado: "Fear doesn't want you to make the journey to the mountain if he can rattle you enough; fear will persuade you to take your eyes off the peaks and settle for a dull existence in the flatlands."

Even though Bobby didn't come, I sent him the verse Jeremiah 29:11, which is important for everyone! I believe even Trent said this is one of his favorites!

"For I know the plans I have for you, declared the Lord, plans to prosper you and not to harm you, plans to give you hope and a future."

I told Bobby to trust God and that He has big plans for us. I know you cannot see it because of our circumstances, but I can see the brighter days ahead!

That evening around 9:15 p.m. I shared Turning Page by Sleeping At Last with Bobby via Spotify, which is our other love song. He is my turning page. I love him so much. I died a thousand years waiting for him and would die a thousand more for him.

Monday

Today was the Awards ceremony at school. Bobby came and sat next to me to watch the students and Lucas receive awards for the school year. Lucas received recognition for being on the honor roll for the last 9 weeks and for all year long! He seemed proud of himself, and we were proud of him, too!

Bobby wasn't very talkative today. He seemed to be in a bad mood or like something was bugging him. I took the day off dashing because I had a counseling appointment and then the ceremony, and I was tired, too. While resting, I came across a meme and saved it. Of course, I couldn't help myself, so I sent it to my husband. The meme stated that marriage is not about a beautiful wedding, fancy homes, cute kids, nice cars, and white picket fences. Marriage is hospital stays, working long hours, fighting through struggles, paying bills, keeping the faith, and staying together through it all. I said, "I love you, and I made a vow to be with you for richer or poorer, for better or worse, in sickness and health. In good times and bad. Every moment.

Wednesday 6/12/24

I worked from 10 to 3 today. I had a lot of orders from McDonald's, believe it or not. At least this McDonald's had their act together; maybe it was good management. Or a good team? Who knows. I called Bobby and spoke to him briefly about meeting him later with me and Lucas for dinner somewhere and asked if he preferred Mexican or Asian. He chose Asian. Well, come to think of it, I remembered while trying to recall the Japanese steakhouse that we went to on one of our first dates together. I found it. It was Kyoto in Chesapeake. This was the place where I first told Bobby I loved him.

Well, when we got there, we had to wait for their doors to open. We came right at their opening time. We sat down and looked at the menu, and I asked him if he remembered the restaurant. He said of course you would bring me here and tried to hide his smile. We all ordered steak and rice. I was the only one that caught the shrimp, lol. I wasn't expecting to, though! Dinner was pleasant! We had a good time together.

Just the three of us.

I mentioned that we should go camping this summer, and he responded, "We'll see." It was better than No. We were stuffed! Before leaving, I gave Bobby a pile of mail that had been accumulating from my mom's house. Bobby hugged and kissed me. I told him I loved him, and he said it back: progress. Lucas never liked leaving his dad. He always stretched out his goodbyes. Bobby was Lucas's best friend. I know Lucas loves me, but his dad is his best friend and hero. He loves his dad to death.

Father's Day weekend

I had been working nonstop, dashing. I'd make enough money in one dash to get gas for the next dash. Then I'd make enough money to get something to eat and so forth.

My time had come when my friend told me I had a few weeks to leave their house and find somewhere else to go, so I had to find a room to rent. My search began. After Saturday night, I dashed about all day, and I was exhausted. It was just like any other regular job. Driving around was tiring, and getting in and out of my vehicle and climbing apartment staircases was taxing.

So, I decided to end my dash somewhat early, get some garlic parmesan wings, and watch Bridgerton season 3, part 2. I loved Bridgerton. I was a sucker for any type of British show or film. I loved Jane Austin's Pride & Prejudice, especially the version with Keira Knightly; she was lovely in that film. Who knows, maybe it is my English heritage/ European background that brings me such a passion for British things.

I skipped service on Father's Day and decided to work in the morning. Then proceeded to pick up Lucas from Bobby. I got Lucas to sign the card I got him for his dad and gave him the present to give to him. It wasn't much. They were just a few items from the dollar tree, to be honest. Nitro coffee, candy, beard oil, tea tree face wash, some lotion, and a couple of other things. Just a little gift; it's the thought that counts. Of course, I wanted to do more, much more. I feel like Bobby deserves more than just that.

I will continue to pray for my husband, show him the love of Christ, be a good wife, fight for him, and keep our family together. Bobby has been through so much, and he deserves the world. I want to make it up to him to create new and happy memories together. I want to give him the best.

I will continue to persevere each and every day, even if it may not be a good day or if it is a hard day. We all go through seasons. One thing is for sure: this year, I know that my faith is back, and my faith has grown stronger. And I know that I can do all things in which Christ strengthens me. Amen.

Hallelujah! Praise the Lord!

JESUS IS OUR LIGHTHOUSE

I am going to end with this: when the devil comes knocking on your door, and demons attack, get on your knees and pray! Have a good support system! Please, whatever you do, do not isolate yourself! No matter how you are feeling or whatever you are thinking, talk to someone or get professional help!! Listen to inspirational speakers and listen to good, wholesome music that lifts your soul! You matter!!! You are meant to be here! Just like Trent Shelton says, "Know your worth"! You are loved by an amazing God! You are loved and cherished by someone in the world! Everything you do in this world means something!

I have the semi-colon tattooed on my left wrist, and it says LIVE. The semi-colon represents life continuance! In a sentence, it means continuance. Even though we may be going through a storm, there is always calm after the storm. Life continues. Life is precious. Sailors on ships used to depend on lighthouses a lot to return home from long voyages from the sea. They would look for the light through the huge waves and the dim fog.

Matthew 8, 23-27 says, "Then he got into the boat, and his disciples followed him. Suddenly, a furious storm came up on the lake, and the waves swept over the boat. But Jesus was sleeping. The disciples went and woke him, saying, "Lord, save us! We're going to drown!" He replied, "You of little faith, why are you so afraid?" Then he got up and rebuked the winds and the waves, and it was completely calm."

When we are going through life's storms and trials, we tend to lose our faith in God and lose our focus on Jesus, our lighthouse. When we do this, we begin to sink. Everything around us begins to crumble, and that is when the enemy loves to come in and attack us the most. It is our choice to sink or swim! It is vital to keep our eyes on Jesus, our lighthouse, all of the time, but especially during the storms! He is our lifeguard and savior and the only one that can save you from drowning!

Does everyone remember the What Would Jesus Do Movement? Okay, well, if you're too young to remember, I'll give you a little backstory. The WWJD phrase came from a popular book called *In His Steps: What Would Jesus Do?* by Charles Sheldon. Anyway, the phrase became popular again in the 1990s and appeared on wristbands that people wore as a symbol to promote a movement to demonstrate the love of Jesus Christ.

Jesus Christ gave his life for me on the cross, and I want to do my best to live for Jesus.

Everything that I do in my life is ultimately to glorify God. I really want people to recognize Jesus for his Hebrew name, Yehoshua, or the shorter version, Yeshua. When I picture myself with him, I always picture myself in a white gown on the beach, dancing and smiling in pure joy, just pure joy. I worship him in that way.

This isn't the end; it is only the beginning! I want to start a new movement! Everything that I am and everything that I do, I want to do for Jesus!

So, my movement is:

"I am doing it for Yeshua!"

ABOUT THE AUTHOR

Samantha Reed Bond is a writer from Suffolk, Virginia. She's a graduate from ECPI University and holds a B.S. degree in Healthcare Administration. Her passion for writing began as a young teenager and developed further and she published poetry while attending Tidewater Community College prior. "Sarcoma: The Demon Inside" is her first book to be published.

When Sam is not writing, she's found working hard for her family, attending church, reading or painting. Sam is also passionate about mental health awareness and helping others with their spiritual walk and salvation. She's currently pursuing her M.A. degree in Spiritual Formation at Regent University.